COWBOY
Marshal

Cowboy Hero, Book 6

BARBARA MCMAHON

Cowboy Marshal
Copyright © 2016 Barbara McMahon
All Rights Reserved

No part of this book may be used or reproduced in any manner whatsoever without written permission from the author except in the case of brief quotations embodied in critical articles or reviews.

This is a work of fiction. Names, characters, places and incidents are products of the author's imagination and are used fictitiously. Any resemblance to actual events, locales, organizations or persons living or dead is entirely coincidental.

One

Savannah saw him as soon as she exited the jet way. He was impossible to miss since the waiting area was empty—except for him. The other passengers from the plane hurried to baggage claim or connecting flights. The seats in the departure lounge were empty. The gate at the end of the concourse was deserted. She and her two escorts were the last to disembark. Only the flight crew remained behind.

In front of her, casually leaning against the ticket counter, stood Rowdy Yates, Wyatt Earp and Matt Dillon, all rolled up into one. He wasn't as tall as the two men flanking her, but tall enough, at least six feet. Even with her high heels, she only topped out at five-six. In her bare feet she stood three inches shorter. Six feet loomed large in comparison.

At first glance, she thought he was a cowboy. His boots were scuffed and rundown at the heel. His jeans were faded, white thread showing at the seams, at the knees and—She jerked her gaze upward. The blue chambray shirt covered broad shoulders, muscular arms. His dark hat tilted back at a rakish angle. For a brief second she wondered if he was an official greeter for the State of Colorado. He could be a poster model for cowboy.

But his eyes gave him away. Dark brown, they constantly scanned the area, assessing, weighing, *anticipating*. When they focused on her, she felt as if he'd touched her. The shocking sensation quivered through her as she drew closer.

She should be used to it. She'd been scrutinized by a dozen men like him in the last five months. Her life had turned topsy-turvey and she wondered if things would ever return to normal.

There was something different about him and she wasn't sure she liked it. It was almost a physical sense of touch. She hadn't felt any kind of physical response to the others. They were merely men assigned to guard her, to keep her safe.

What was different about this one? Maybe nothing, maybe it was fatigue.

He glanced away, but she knew he'd memorized her every feature. The two men beside her didn't even pause as they drew even with the man.

"Second rest room," he said barely above a whisper, his lips scarcely moving, his gaze going beyond her, down the empty jet way. If she hadn't been expecting it, she'd have missed it. But she was getting good at picking up things she'd never noticed before.

Abject terror had a way of honing the senses.

Without acknowledgment, the men beside her maintained their pace.

"Is he the new marshal?" Savannah Adams asked as she hurried to keep up.

They rarely shortened their stride and her own didn't begin to match theirs. For months she'd been trying to keep up.

Of course, they had reasons to hurry. They were trying

to get her hidden safely away—to save her life. Every second in the open left her that much more exposed.

She'd been handed off from one set of strangers to another during the last two days. She'd flown more hours than most pilots did in a month, had passed back and forth between time zones, skipped meals and sleep—all in the effort to confuse and lose any pursuers.

She was tired, grimy and thoroughly disgusted with the turn of events. Now the new man didn't even greet her. Despite her fear, she was fast growing tired of the cloak-and-dagger routine. She just wanted to turn back the clock and go back to her safe, normal life!

Maybe she guessed wrong. Maybe he wasn't the next marshal assigned to watch her for the next few weeks, until time for the trial where she would be the primary witness.

He certainly didn't look like the others. They wore suits, he looked as if he'd just come from the range. The others were tall, silent, and all looked alike in their short hair and dark suits. He had looked different—tanned, fit. *Sexy.*

She shook her head and rubbed her eyes. They were gritty from lack of sleep. She ached with fatigue. Even so, that was no reason to fantasize about some tall stranger standing at the gate.

Savannah had seen her share of gorgeous men and with a lot more tanned, sexy bodies showing than she'd seen on that cowboy. The young men who strutted the beaches in Miami wearing skimpy bathing suits were justifiably proud of their fine physiques. Sleek and muscular, tanned and fit, the endless parade lost its fascination years ago.

Now some cowboy decked out in jeans and a shirt

sparked her interest. She was obviously too tired to make any sense.

Yet she knew she'd sure sit up and take notice if that cowboy strutted by!

"We'll wait here, Miss Adams," one of the marshals said.

Was it Bruce Champion? She couldn't remember all the names. They began to blur in her mind along with the faces. She was so tired, she just wanted to lie down and sleep for a week.

"Good luck," the second one said, turning to scan the faces of the passengers milling in the busy concourse of the Denver airport.

She entered the ladies' rest room. She could wash her face to try to shake some of the fatigue. How long before she could sleep in a bed?

"Savannah Adams?" A woman about her age and general appearance walked over, glancing over her shoulder at the almost deserted area by the sinks. Only a mother and her little girl were washing hands.

"Yes." A clutch of fear stabbed her.

Glancing behind her, she saw the way was clear if she turned and dashed out.

"Marshal Sally Montgomery."

The woman carefully handed Savannah her identification, her body shielding it from view of the woman at the sink.

It took a couple of seconds for Savannah to focus on the picture, to read the information by the badge. Satisfied the woman was a marshal, she nodded and handed the wallet back. The jolt of adrenaline drove away the last vestiges of fatigue as splashing water on her face never would have. She was wide awake and alert.

Once the woman and her daughter left, Sally said, "Come with me. The last stall on the second row is for handicapped. We can both fit in it."

Puzzled, Savannah followed her.

"I don't suppose they told you the plan," Sally asked quietly as she hurried Savannah into the last stall and closed the door. No one had seen them both enter the same stall.

Savannah shook her head. "What plan?"

It was a tight squeeze in the stall. What now?

"We change clothes. When I leave, I walk away with Bruce and Doug. You wait two minutes then follow. Mike Black will be waiting. He's in charge of you in this district."

"Mike Black? What does he look like?"

Savannah began to unbutton her jacket. More subterfuge. She should be used to it by now, but she wasn't. Normalcy was something to be cherished if she ever regain it.

"About six feet tall, dark hair." Sally grinned at Savannah. "He was the hunk standing by the gate when you got off the plane. He wanted to make sure he knew you when you came out of here. Hurry up. We don't have much time. We don't think anyone followed you this far, but I don't want to raise any doubts by taking too long."

Swiftly the two women changed clothes. Gone was her trendy cherry red suit, the short skirt which showed off her legs, the vee of her jacket displaying a hint of cleavage.

Instead, Savannah donned a pair of faded jeans. Tight faded jeans. And a loose-fitting cotton shirt that buttoned up the front and whose sleeves she rolled up above her wrists.

"Pull your hair back," Sally said, brushing and teasing her

own until it swirled around her face in a parody of Savannah's usual style.

"We don't really look that much alike," Savannah commented as she complied, reaching for the rubber band Sally handed her.

"Our hair color's about the same. And I'll wear sunglasses when I leave. We aren't sure there's anyone out there watching, but just in case, I think this'll fool them long enough to let you and Mike get away. That's the best we can hope for if you've been followed. With a bit of luck, you lost any tails a couple of flights ago. Ready?"

Savannah nodded. The entire last six months seemed surreal. This was merely one more facet in a world turned upside down.

"As I'll ever be, I guess," she said.

Sally grinned. "Don't worry, Mike's the best He's never lost a witness yet. I wouldn't mind trading places with you. Three weeks with one of the area's most eligible bachelors! Wow, lucky you."

Savannah smiled politely and nodded. The smile faded as Sally left.

Savannah leaned against the cool tile wall, the silence in the rest room pounding in her ear. Lucky her. She'd witnessed a murder, there were men trying to find her to make sure she couldn't testify, She hadn't been home in over five months. And because of her, another person had been injured when the "safe house" in Key Biscayne had been discovered and someone tried to blow it up.

Her friends must be frantic wondering where she was.

And she was worried about her shop. She'd been manager for several years, had been in the negotiation stage of buying into the business. Had that plan been put in jeopardy?

She had no family to worry about her, or for her to worry about, that was the only lucky aspect about the whole situation.

"You're still alive," she whispered. "That's lucky."

She glanced at her watch. Several minutes had passed. Taking a deep breath, she walked out. And almost ran smack into Mike Black.

"Thought I was going to have to come in after you," he said, throwing his arm around her shoulder and turning her toward the terminal. Urging her away from the rest room as if they were late.

"Shouldn't I ask for identification?" she said, feeling breathless with the pace he set, with his touch, his proximity. His heat enveloped her. His arm rested heavy on her shoulders, hard and strong and with a tingling that charged through her which had nothing to do with fatigue.

Here was a man who vowed to protect her, make sure she made it through the next several weeks until time for the trial.

Something convinced her she'd be safe. And for a moment her legs wobbled with relief.

"Smart girl, but not here. Didn't Sally tell you how to recognize me?"

"Actually I recognized you when we left the plane. Only I thought good guys wore white hats."

Mike's dark felt cowboy hat tipped low over his forehead, shielding his eyes from others, making it easier for him to observe without anyone knowing exactly where he looked.

"That's Hollywood. Nowadays bad guys wear white hats trying to fool the world. Have a good flight?" he asked as they left the concourse and melded into the busy terminal.

They threaded their way through the throngs of people greeting arriving passengers or bidding teary farewells to friends and loved ones. Dodging those who staggered beneath luggage they swore they could carry on the planes, and the ones looking tired and hungry after a long flight, Mike kept moving toward the exit. While he set a fast pace, he didn't push them fast enough to raise suspicion.

"Which flight? We left Miami sometime Tuesday. I've seen more airports than I ever wanted. Flown more miles than most people do in a lifetime. And I didn't even get frequent flier miles for it."

He pulled her out of the way of a harried, determined man bent on making his way through the throng without regard for anyone else. Mike's eyes constantly swept the churning crowd.

"Uh-oh." Mike pulled her to one side, wrapped his arms around her, leaned over and covered her mouth with his.

Savannah caught her breath, her eyes still open in shocked surprise. His lips were warm and firm as they pressed gently against hers. The brim of his hat enclosed them, she felt almost hidden. Slowly he revolved until her back pressed against the wall. Sheltered from the crowd by his body, she was too stunned to move. She could only stand stock-still in his arms and feel. Feel the heat from his body ignite hers. Feel the strength in his arms as they bound her close to him. Feel the strange pulsing awareness of the intimacy of the kiss as time stood still and she spun away in a world of fantastic make-believe.

Men had told her she was pretty. They'd complimented her light blond hair, her blue eyes, and the flawless complexion she owed to her maternal grandmother.

But no one had ever fallen so hard and fast that they had to kiss her within minutes of meeting her.

Mike pulled back a little, his eyes serious. He looked at her face for a moment, then scanned the area. "Come on."

He released her, grabbed her hand and pulled her to a door marked "No Admittance." Slipping behind it, he hurried her along the empty hallway.

"Wait just a darn minute." She tried to catch her breath. She wanted some answers.

"Not now, Miss Adams, I don't want to waste a minute."

Miss Adams? From intimacy to formality in one stroke?

"I don't think it's wasting anything if I get a few answers." She was having trouble talking and breathing at the quick pace he set.

He slowed marginally and nodded, glancing once behind them at the empty hallway.

"What do you want to know?"

"That kiss for starters—"

"I thought someone spotted you and I wanted to see what happened if we stopped for a while. Besides, it fits in with the cover we've devised."

"And that is?" She drew in a ragged breath. The corridor seemed endless.

For a moment he hesitated, then shrugged. "We are going to stay on a ranch. And everyone there thinks we're engaged."

"Engaged! Are you nuts? We can't be engaged, we just met."

"It's a cover story, Miss Adams, not reality. We spend the next three weeks at a ranch where no one knows you're a witness in hiding. Everyone thinks you're my fiancée"

"That's it? That's your grand plan to keep me safe until it's time to testify?"

She stopped and yanked her hand from his grasp.

He stopped, looked back at her and slowly smiled. "That's it."

Savannah's heart flopped. He had a dimple in his left cheek!

She stared, mesmerized. Besides being drop-dead gorgeous, masculine in an old-fashioned way she didn't often see in Miami, being sexy as could be—*he had a dimple*!

She was a sucker for dimples and realized she was in danger. More danger than just some crooks from Miami trying to silence her. She was in danger of losing what sanity remained if she hung around this cowboy for any length of time.

And she had no time in her life for a relationship, especially one with a man who lived two thousand miles from home and probably ate women like her for breakfast. She had her life planned out and it didn't include getting married anytime soon.

Not that there was a chance of that. This was a charade, a cover to keep her safe. That was all.

Four minutes later they were outside moving through the cool morning air. In the distance Savannah saw the silhouette of downtown Denver. To the left in the distance rose the first range of the Rockies. Stopping in wonder, she pulled her hand free again and stared, her eyes drinking in every gorgeous peak.

"What?" He looked around, instantly alert.

Seeing nothing out of the ordinary, he looked back at her.

"The Rocky Mountains! Right there!"

She pointed, danger and fatigue temporarily forgotten in the delight of seeing the famous mountain range. The distant rugged peaks were snow-covered. The closer ones softer, more rounded, covered with trees. In the crystal clear Colorado air, she stretched out her fingers, feeling as if she could touch them.

"Miss Adams, those mountains have been there for eons, they'll continue to be there long after you and I have departed this earth. We don't have to stare at them now. But if you're so interested in them, you will be pleased to learn we will be right in the heart of the Rockies in only a little while. Come on. If I did see someone interested in you back there we don't want to hang around waiting for them to find us."

"Did you see someone after me?" she asked, turning to follow.

Again she had to almost run to keep up. What was with these marshals? Did they all compete in two marathons before breakfast? Couldn't any of them walk at a normal pace?

"Can't be sure. Someone was sure studying you. Of course it could be because of how you look." He ran his gaze over her once again, his lips tightening.

"And just how do I look?" she asked breathlessly. "While you're thinking up an answer, could we slow down?"

He stopped. "We'll be in the car in a few minutes. You can rest all you want after that. We've got a three-hour drive ahead of us."

"Where're we going now?" she asked, gulping in the thin air. "Denver can't be that far, isn't that it over there?" She gestured to the skyline of high-rise buildings to the south.

"Wyoming."

"Wyoming?" Stunned, Savannah stared at him.

She lived in Miami Beach. She knew nothing about cowboys and ranches and wide-open spaces. She loved the beach, liked lying in the sun, swimming in the buoyant ocean waters. Liked the casual lifestyle in the warm southern city.

Wyoming sounded like a place she didn't want to visit. The air here was noticeably cooler than Florida. It was May—when did it get hot in Colorado? In Wyoming?

"Couldn't we go to Southern California instead?" she asked hopefully. That'd be much more her style. Newport Beach or even San Diego.

Turning, Mike took her shoulders in his hands and leaned over until he gazed deep into her eyes.

"We aren't on a vacation junket. You're under the protection of the United States Marshal's Service until after Joel Ramirez's trial. After the fiasco in Key Biscayne, I'd think you'd insist we do a better job. I plan to do just that."

"You're the best, Sally said," she murmured, mesmerized by the pull of attraction.

His eyes were dark, piercing, intent. His strong jaw hinted at stubbornness. She knew instantly he wasn't a man to give in to a witness's whims. Not that any of the others had, either, though they had been a bit more diplomatic about things.

She felt sure she could be just as safe in Southern California where it was warm, as she would be in Wyoming.

Especially on a ranch. Especially posing as this man's fiancée.

"I'll do my job. And this time, no one will find you. You can count on it," he vowed.

"You might say I've bet my life on it," she replied.

The fear that swamped her was familiar. It had been with her for months. She'd done nothing but be in the wrong place at the wrong time, and now she lived in constant anxiety.

After two aborted attempts on her life, she'd come to rely on others to keep her safe. She didn't like it, but she had little choice if she wanted to stay alive.

Mike's grim expression softened, a smile displayed that devastating dimple. As he straightened, he brushed the backs of his fingers across her cheek in a comforting caress totally unexpected from such a tough man.

"I'm going to do my best to keep you safe. You can stop worrying and relax. Look on this as a vacation. A lot of people pay money to stay on an authentic cattle ranch, you get to do so courtesy of Uncle Sam."

"We're staying on a ranch," she repeated.

The thought of Denver had been bad enough, but at least it was a fair-sized city. She didn't know a thing about ranches, or horses, or cows. She liked trendy little restaurants, coffee bars, the beach.

"I'm not sure a ranch is the best place—" she started to say.

"I'll explain everything once we're in the Jeep. Let's go."

He took her hand and hurried her through the service vehicles until they reached the parking lot. In no time they were climbing into a dusty, battered Jeep. When Mike started the engine, it instantly roared to throaty life, its power evident.

Leaving Denver International Airport behind him, Mike turned the Jeep north and in seconds they were in the midst of flat open plains—cattle country.

"I don't have a thing to my name," Savannah said as she realized Bruce still had her tote bag. It contained all she'd carried with her the last two days.

"We'll stop in Laramie and get some clothes. Sally'll keep your bag until it's time to return to Miami," Mike said, his eyes scanning the rear-view mirror before he looked ahead.

"I must say I expected a cop to drive something besides a Jeep. A black Mustang, maybe," she murmured, looking at the battered vehicle.

"This is more suitable for where we're heading. It's got an engine in it that won't quit. And if anything goes down, we can cut across country in this baby."

"I really don't want to go to a ranch," she said firmly. Surely she had some rights in this.

"Sorry, but it's the best I could do on such short notice. We're trying to avoid usual methods and safe houses in this case. There's a suspicion that there's been a leak somewhere. The discovery of the safe house in Florida could have been a coincidence, but we're not sure. No one knows where we're going but my immediate boss."

"Going to a ranch is safe?"

"I've officially taken vacation. The ranch belongs to my brother. There's no reason for anyone to know that's where I'm heading. And we'll have the added protection of the men who work on the ranch."

"Your brother doesn't mind?"

"Actually he and my sister-in-law aren't there. They just married and are on their honeymoon. We'll have the house to ourselves."

Great. He kisses like a million dollars, flashes that adorable dimple and then tells her they'd be alone. Just the two of them. In the middle of the Wyoming wilderness.

Forgotten was the reason she was there. Forgotten was the fear of the last few months, the worry about her boutique, her career. Blazing before her hovered the thought that she and Mike Black would be alone in a house reeking with new love with his brother's recent marriage.

She didn't like the setup at all.

"Devotion to duty above and beyond, Marshal. Taking your work home with you," she murmured, her heart tripping in her chest, her hands locked together as she tried to control the wild thoughts that careened around her mind.

"Actually no one there knows it's work. They think I'm coming home with my fiancée."

"Can't beat that for cover, can you?" she muttered, wondering when her heart rate would slow to normal. Wondering when her active imagination would worry about her future and stop remembering the brief kiss at the airport.

"Something wrong with the plan, Miss Adams?"

"Apart from the fact I am not your fiancée, that I know nothing about you, and what I've seen so far I'm not sure I like, there's still the question of suitability. You and I wouldn't suit in a thousand years. How do you plan to pass that off to all the cowboys on the ranch? I can't believe this."

Savannah stared out the windshield, totally amazed at the thought of posing as Mike's fiancée. Rubbing her eyes, she wished for the millionth time she hadn't gone out for a late-night snack two weeks before last Christmas. If she'd stayed home, she'd never have seen Joel Ramirez and his gun. Or the man he murdered in cold blood.

Now she was stuck with some wild west character, pretending to be engaged of all things.

Kisses. Engaged couples kissed a lot. She felt a flush as she imagined how romantic they needed to appear to fool everybody.

Would he kiss her again?

She'd been shocked at his kiss at the airport, next time she'd be prepared. Prepared? To have her socks knocked off?

Touching. Engaged couples touched a lot. Most of her friends in the throes of love couldn't keep their hands off each other.

She darted a quick glance at Mike's hands as they held the steering wheel. Large, strong, capable. What would they feel like caressing her? His fingers had been gentle when he brushed her cheek earlier.

Her temperature rose another notch at the thought of his hands doing more than brushing across her cheek.

"I don't think so," she said.

"Don't misunderstand, Miss Adams, you don't have a choice in this. It's the way I think I can best keep you safe and that's the way it'll be." His tone brooked no argument.

She slumped back against the seat, defeated. Everything over the last several months had been taken out of her hands. Used to being in charge of her life, she didn't like having her every decision made by someone else. She'd been on her own since a teenager. She'd run the high end boutique in Miami Beach for the past several years, increased their customer base, boosted sales.

If she could come up with a better idea, maybe Mike Black would consider it.

Except somehow she didn't think he'd like her idea of lounging on the beach in San Diego.

Almost too tired to think straight, she slowly closed her eyes. If she rested for a few minutes, she'd surely be able to come up with some alternative. Wasn't that why she was being considered as a possible partner at the boutique, because of her innovative ideas? Surely she could think of something that'd appeal to Mr. Know-it-all Marshal Mike Black.

When Savannah tilted toward the door, Mike glanced over. She'd fallen asleep. Her head pressed against the window, her hands relaxed in her lap, resting on the taut jeans that molded her figure like they'd been painted on.

He shook his head, glancing in the rear-view minor to make sure no one followed. Until she could testify at the trial, she was his responsibility and he took that seriously. No one was going to get to her on his watch.

He glanced at her again. Asleep, she looked young and tired and very pretty. There was no question she was a knockout. He'd seen the photos and they didn't begin to do her justice. Black and white hadn't captured the golden sheen to her hair. Nor how soft it looked. Clenching his fingers around the wheel, he tried to ignore the stab of interest that seeing her engendered. She was a case, a person to keep from harm.

But the way that red skirt had hugged her hips when she'd disembarked from the plane had his eyes dropping to follow their swaying rhythm. The skirt hadn't been tight precisely, but it sure fit snugly, defining her soft curves like a caress.

And that mane of wavy and curly blond hair that swung in the same tempo, still enticed even drawn back into a ponytail. What would it feel like running through his fingers?

He'd thought Sally and Savannah a close enough match after he'd seen Savannah Adams's picture to pull off the switch. Reality proved Sally just a shade slimmer. Not that her jeans suffered from being worn by Savannah Adams. Far from it. When she'd exited that rest room, he'd hardly been able to stop staring.

He had to stifle the urge to have her walk a dozen steps in front of him so he could watch the soft sway of her hips, like he'd done when she'd worn that sexy red number.

He'd read her file when it'd been faxed to the office last week. He knew she managed some trendy boutique in the heart of Miami Beach's tourist district. He knew, too, that she had a definite flare for fashion and a distinctive style of her own. Just looking at her would have convinced him.

When she'd disembarked from the airplane, he'd seen solid evidence of that flare. From her tousled hair, to the discreet makeup she wore, to the red suit that had clung to every curve like a lover's hand, every inch of her proclaimed a blatant femininity that'd drive a man wild.

And it'd been a long time since he'd had even the smallest twinge of interest in a woman. Now attraction almost shot off the scale.

He frowned as he flicked another glance in the rear-view mirror. No one followed them. After all the efforts of the marshal's office, there shouldn't be anyone within five states interested in Savannah Adams. He'd probably erred on the side of caution when he saw the man studying Savannah at the airport.

When he'd realized that man was staring at her, he'd reacted instinctively, kissing her long enough to give the man time to pass if he proved to be an innocent bystander. Mike had watched from the corner of his eyes as the man walked by.

The kiss had been a mistake. Or at least his reaction to that kiss had been a mistake. A big mistake. And he didn't like making mistakes.

How was he to know how soft and feminine she'd feel? How was he to know that pressing his lips against hers would awaken long dormant desire and needs he'd thought long gone? How was he to know he'd react like a drowning man to her perfume or that her heat would ignite a blaze of his own?

She was a witness to a violent crime under his protection until the trial. Nothing more.

He questioned if her assessment of his idea for a cover story had been right on target. How was he going to pretend to be engaged and maintain his distance? Living together in close proximity would be more dangerous to his own mental health than physically dangerous because of the men trying to kill her.

And he needed to stay close, to make sure no one else got close.

But engaged? Dumb idea from the get-go.

He considered his options. Could he get her interested in things at the ranch? They'd ride horses, join the cowboys with the chores and watch television in the evening. It was only three weeks, twenty-one days. He'd been in much worse situations, more dangerous. All he had to do was remind himself she was under his protection. He could handle anything for three weeks.

Slowly the faint scent of honeysuckle permeated the Jeep. It was subtle, elusive, but definitely honeysuckle. He drew a deep breath. She'd smelled like honeysuckle when he'd kissed her. Her skin had been soft against his mouth, her fragrance filled his senses even as her soft body filled his arms. He'd tried to stay alert to possible danger, but for a split second he'd lost himself in the armful of sweet woman.

Now the scent teased his senses again. He remembered with vivid clarity the feel of her in his arms.

It looked like ti was going to be a very long three weeks! He wondered if there was any chance of moving up the trial date. He'd ask when he checked in.

Savannah stirred and opened her eyes. Her neck ached, her right arm felt numb. Slowly she sat up and shook her head to come wide awake. The Jeep was stopped at a traffic light.

"Where are we?" she asked slowly, looking around at the one-story buildings, at the tall leafy trees that lined the street, the profusion of lilacs in full bloom along the wall of the brick building on the corner.

"Laramie. I planned to wake you in a couple of minutes. We'll do some quick shopping, then head for the ranch."

When the light turned green, he turned left, into the local Shop'n Save parking lot. He found a spot near the main door, pulled in and stopped.

Savannah looked at the store, then looked at him.

"I'll wait here," she said, still feeling groggy from sleeping so long.

"'Fraid not. We're shopping for you. I don't have a clue to your size. Come on."

She swung her gaze around to the store, as dismay dawned. "You can't think I would buy clothes there? I haven't bought anything at a discount store in—a long time. I usually shop at—"

"You usually shop in Miami Beach. This is Laramie, Wyoming. I want to get you to the ranch as quickly as possible. I don't have time to be traipsing all over town while you decide if a store is fancy enough for you. We're heading for a working ranch. You can grab a few pairs of jeans, a couple of shirts and you'll be set. Come on."

She blinked at his rough voice and slid from the Jeep. Holding on to her self control, she raised her chin and followed along, silent, but seething. She hadn't asked to be assigned to him, he could have been a bit more understanding of her circumstances.

And she didn't want to buy clothes from the local discount house. She'd worked hard to put her past behind her and had sworn the first day on the job at the boutique to buy the best.

Walking into the store made her feel as if she were sixteen again, dirt poor, and no where else to go. She didn't like the feeling or the memories.

When they reached the women's department, she smiled. Mike Black looked totally out of place, a big rugged male surrounded by feminine apparel.

Revenge flowed sweet as imp of mischief took hold. Trust a man to think all clothes were the same. Sighing softly, she began to look with some interest at the display racks. She had no choice and it was only temporary. She could make the best of the situation.

Not that she was going to tell him that. How long could she stretch out this shopping expedition?

"I'll need underwear," she murmured, heading for lingerie.

Lacy teddies and slips, sheer panties and bras surrounded them. Watching from the corner of her eye, Savannah grew smugly satisfied when he resettled his hat, pulling it low on his forehead as if to shelter himself from the amused looks of the other customers in the department—all women.

Serves him right, she thought, looking for a brand name she recognized, any name would do. Nothing she saw compared with the underwear she'd left behind. The mad dash from the safe house had saved her life, but nothing but the suit she'd been wearing had been saved.

"Find what you need and let's get going," he growled, dogging her footsteps, glaring at the other shoppers.

"I don't know if the styles—"

"Savannah!"

She jumped and looked up at him. It was the first time he'd called her by her first name.

"What?"

Her eyes darted around as fear clutched her heart. Had they been found? Had all the doubling back and furtive changing planes been in vain?

He snagged her gaze, stared into her blue eyes, his narrowed and intent. "Don't play games. I don't have time for that."

She took a breath and reached out to grab a handful of panties. Two steps further and she snagged a couple of bras in her size.

"Now what?" she asked.

He was right. She wanted to reach the ranch as soon as possible. At least it offered safety.

"Jeans. You need jeans. There are no styles to jeans, they come in dark blue, black or stone-washed. That's all. Get some shirts, some jeans, socks and let's go!"

"Gee, I see shopping with you is a really fun event. What do you do, order your clothes by catalog?" she muttered as she marched over to the rack of blue jeans. It took her a couple of minutes to find her size. She took three pairs. "Do I get to try them on?"

"Yeah, but get everything else, too, so you can try everything on at the same time."

Impatience seethed from him. He made no effort to contain it. He scanned the other shoppers. No one looked out of place. He'd recognize anyone who didn't belong. A paid assassin would stick out here as much as he did.

Savannah rolled her eyes and walked over to the shirts and tops. The clothes were certainly different from the ones she bought and displayed for Fashion Image. Plain cotton, serviceable, totally different from the sophisticated styles she was used to. She resented having to purchase them, but she couldn't wear Sally's clothes for three weeks. She had to wear something.

For a moment she remembered all the lovely outfits in her closet. She didn't have a great deal, but what she had was expensive and elegant. When she'd landed her job at the boutique, she'd vowed never to shop in a discount store like this again.

So much for self-made promises, she thought grimly.

"I suppose it'd be too much to ask if they carried silk blouses," she said as she studied the cotton shirts and ribbed tops.

"It'd be too much for a cattle ranch, that's for darn sure," Mike ground out.

If this was an indication of how things were going to go for the next three weeks, it'd be worse than he thought.

Her body looked like an angel, but there was nothing angelic about her temperament, it was enough to try a saint.

"Would you hurry up?"

She turned and smiled brightly up at him. "Do you want to see the things as I try them on?" she asked, her eyes wide, her smile almost blinding.

"No! Just make sure they fit and let's go. I give you ten minutes."

"Grumpy," she said clearly, heading for the small fitting room. Would she really last three weeks with Mike Black? He was bossy and hardheaded and didn't care a thing about what she wanted.

Yet what choice did she have? She had to make do, she'd run out of options.

Two

Savannah stormed into the dressing room ready to scream. Tall, dark and dimpled or not, she wasn't falling for some dumb macho cowboy-type in the wild, wild west. She liked the sophisticated pleasures of Miami Beach. And she definitely didn't like jeans. She didn't like orders and she was sure she wouldn't like Marshal Mike Black upon better acquaintance.

Tugging on a second pair of jeans, she held her breath while she zipped them. They were snug. She bent over and moved around. Not that tight—they didn't bind or cut into her. And they'd keep her warm in the cool mountain air.

With a sigh, Savannah reached up and pulled the rubber band from her hair, running her fingers through it to fluff it up. Rummaging in her purse, which Sally had thankfully left her, she found a comb and pulled it through, tugging and styling until she was finally satisfied. There, she looked normal. Well, except for the clothes.

She unbuttoned the shirt another notch, caught the ends and knotted them above her waist. Tilting her head, she studied herself in the mirror. Better, but still not herself. It seemed more like she might have appeared if she hadn't left home so long ago. If she hadn't been so determined to make a success of herself and succeeded. It would have to do. Maybe a scarf or something for a bit of flair.

Who was she kidding? There was no way she could dress up the outfit. She'd do better to give in gracefully and play cowgirl for a while. At least no one she knew would see her here.

"Okay, Marshal Black, here I come," she muttered as she gathered up the new clothes and left the fitting room. She'd included two pairs of shorts and a plain bathing suit. Surely it would warm up enough to keep her tan going. What else was she going to do for the next three weeks?For some reason she didn't consider the possibility of moving again. She somehow knew Mike Black would keep her safe until time for the trial.

Mike stared at her when she came into view. Good grief, she looked as alien to Wyoming as a Martian. Her hair spilled around her shoulders again like a golden cloud. Her cheeks were dusty pink and her eyes looked even bluer than he'd remembered.

The sexy woman who sashayed from the fitting room would give him fits before this assignment ended.

Every woman in the area stopped to look at her, most of them with envy, he noted grimly. Scanning the floor one more time, he assured himself no one appeared overly interested in Savannah Adams beyond the attention she garnered from her looks. And that proved more than enough.

So much for keeping a low profile. He stepped forward.

"Done?" He raked his gaze down, pausing at that tantalizing strip of skin that peeped between the knotted shirt and the top of her jeans, as tanned as her arms. Was she

26

tanned all over?

He wouldn't be surprised.

The thought of finding out nearly drove him crazy.

"Don't I need some boots?" she asked, blinking her eyes at him.

He swore he could feel a breeze from her long lashes. They were dark and curved—the perfect frame for those deep blue eyes. He could almost drown in those eyes.

For a heartbeat he considered calling his boss and asking to be reassigned. Less than four hours into the assignment and he was already thinking thoughts about this sexy package he had no business thinking. This was business and he'd make sure they both remembered it. The memory was all too fresh with what could happen if they forgot. He didn't want a breach of security in Wyoming. Bad enough the safe house in Florida had been targeted.

"Boots would be good," he said. "More than good, necessary where we're headed."

"And a hat. A white hat!" she said firmly.

He nodded, taking her arm and steering her toward the shoe department. The sooner they were done, the better he'd feel. He wanted to reach the ranch as quickly as possible. He was as certain as he could be they hadn't been followed, but no sense taking unnecessary chances.

If a stranger came within a mile of the ranch, he'd know it. It was the safest place he could think of to guard this witness.

Savannah felt his touch to her toes. What was there about this man that made her so aware of him? So aware of the primal attraction that flooded? Was it fear that heightened her senses?

She'd been too busy building her career, carving a niche for herself, to bother with any long-term relationships. In fact, she rarely dated. She'd been burned once and wouldn't repeat that experience.

So why did she feel—almost tuned in to Mike's touch.

Once she found a pair of boots that fit and picked out the perfect cowboy hat, Mike took charge, buying the clothes, and hustling her out of the store as quickly as he could. His eyes constantly scanning the store.

Savannah couldn't forget for a second how her life had been disrupted.

"I feel like I'm the prisoner," she said as they headed for the car. The parking lot was crowded, but no one was paying any attention to them. She wore her new hat. The rest of the clothes and boots were in bags the marshal carried.

He glanced at her. "I'm sorry you feel that way, Miss Adams. I can understand it. In a way, you are. But it's for your own safety."

"I know. It's just I miss being able to do what I want, when I want," she replied. "And I thought you were calling me Savannah. After all, we are engaged."

Tucking her arm in his, she leaned against him as she flirted a little. "And I'll call you Mikie."

She felt his start and smiled. Maybe she wasn't the only one affected by this strange attraction. It was his dumb idea to pretend to be engaged. Maybe she'd make the most of it.

The thought of teasing this serious man was tantalizing. She had nothing else to do to while away the days. And it might prove fun.

"Can we eat before we head for the old homestead, Mikie?" she asked as they walked toward the Jeep.

"It's only another half hour to the ranch. We'll wait," he said, opening the door for her and tossing in the shopping bags. Again his eyes scanned the area. He looked back at her. "And it's Mike. Got it?"

Savannah rubbed her stomach. She should have bought a candy bar in the Shop'n Save. She'd stopped eating airport food yesterday and was starving.

"I'm really hungry," she said.

"It's only another half hour. You can wait that long."

He started the engine and they were off.

True to his word, they turned beneath the high wrought-iron gate of the ranch in less than thirty minutes. The grass on either side of the blacktop drive grew high and green. On the left a score or more cattle grazed on the belly-high grass. Beyond, the steep sides of a mountain began its climb, with the sun poised near its rim. Night would fall early once the sun slipped behind those mountains, Savannah thought, turning to study her temporary home. It was nothing like Florida.

"Does the ranch have a name?" she asked.

There had been fancy scroll work on top of the gate, but nothing like a name.

"The Bar B," he said.

"Barbie? Like the doll?" she exclaimed, turning to look at him in disbelief.

He grimaced. "No, not like the doll. Like a line, or bar, and the letter B for Black."

He shook his head in disgust and muttered, "Barbie!"

"So is this your family ranch or just your brother's? Are you from Wyoming?"

It occurred to her that she knew nothing about her new

fiancé. Her curiosity grew. She needed information fast. For the sake of this cover scam they were trying to pull off, she told herself. So she didn't mess up.

"The ranch is run by my brother Tom. My brother Conner and I invest in it. But apart from occasional visits, we don't have much involvement in the day-to-day operations."

"Conner," she repeated. "How many brothers do you have?"

Mike flicked a glance her way. "Two. Tom's my younger brother. He just married Sarah Laughlin. They were childhood sweethearts. We always knew they'd marry. Conner's the oldest of us, he lives in Cheyenne. He's an assistant district attorney."

"Where did we meet?" she asked.

"What?"

"If I'm supposed to be your fiancée, I should know where we met, shouldn't I? I mean, what if one of the cowboys asked me a question. I'd hate to blow my cover."

"You stay away from the men," he ordered.

"Excuse me, I thought the plan was to pretend we're engaged. Would you keep your true fiancée away from the men? Or would you be trying to assimilate her into your family–ranch and all?"

"If she looked like you, I'd keep her safe under lock and key," he said under his breath, thinking about the ramifications of giving her free rein on the ranch. She should be safe. No one would look for her here. There were a dozen cowboys to notice if anyone unusual showed up.

She was smart and right. If he'd ever been dumb enough to get engaged, he'd definitely want to show his fiancée all aspects of his life.

Not that he planned to follow in his brother's footsteps. Sarah was all right. They'd known her all their lives. But Mike could still remember the heartache of his mother's departure, the confusion and uncertainties of his father's multiple marriages, every one ending in rage and bitterness.

And he never forgot Amy.

Mike Black was a loner and planned to stay that way. Let Tom marry, father children and continue the Black name. His own solitary way made it easier on the soul.

"Are you one of those dark brooding types?" Savannah asked, studying him. "You've gone off into some other dimension just when I wondered when you'd snap out your next order."

"Sooner than you'll probably like," he said. "I've considered the possible danger if you mingle with the ranch hands. I believe it'll be okay."

"Gee, your faith is overwhelming," she said sarcastically.

"Listen up, Savannah Adams. My sole job is to keep you safe until you can testify at the trial. I will do it as I see fit. When I give you an order, you obey it immediately. Ask questions later, debate with me all you want once the crisis is past. Is all that clear?" he said, his eyes holding hers.

"Clear!"

She wanted to salute, but from the serious nature of his tone, she thought that might not be prudent.

She turned away, staring at the house that came into view; at the barn, corrals and outbuildings that spread out before her. Slowly she scanned the surrounding hills, her heart dropping as her gaze trailed over the acres between her and the mountains that rose to the sky.

She'd never lived more than ten minutes from the ocean.

This was vastly different. As far as she could see, the rolling range land spread out before her, with no water, few trees, and no people. Just cattle, grass and snow on the distant mountain peaks. Snow—and it was May.

For a moment she felt a flare of fierce anger at Joel Ramirez and his trigger-happy ways. It hadn't been her fault she'd stumbled into a murder scene when all she'd done was go for some ice cream at the local mini-mart. It wasn't fair her entire life had been disrupted because of an evil man's revenge. She'd had a hard enough life fending for herself since she was eighteen without this added grief.

Railing against fate for circumstances she was unable to change, she remained silent, willing her anger to fade. No sense taking out her frustrations on Mike. He was doing his job and if he succeeded, she'd owe him her life.

Two men ambled out of the barn when Mike stopped the Jeep beside the house. One touched the brim of his hat and continued toward the bunkhouse, the other hurried over to greet Mike.

"Hank, good to see you." Mike climbed out of the Jeep and reached out to shake hands.

"Good to have you here. Tom said you'd be spending a few weeks this time. Plenty to do."

Politely Hank looked over the hood of the Jeep as Savannah walked toward them. She smiled at him and Mike saw the full effect on the foreman.

Dazzled, dazed, and struck dumb.

Was this going to be a typical reaction of men around her? He could understand it, but it wouldn't help matters if he had to fend off amorous cowboys while trying to guard her.

"Darling, this is just the greatest place! I'm so happy to be here at last. Are you going to introduce me to this handsome cowboy? I can't believe we're really here. I want to learn all I can about ranching. I'm sure you can teach me all Mikie can't," Savannah said, smiling up at Hank as she tucked her arm through Mike's and leaned against him.

She hoped she looked natural. It didn't feel natural. It felt hot and sexy and confusing and gave her ideas she'd never had before. What did engaged couples do when alone?

If he wanted to pretend they were engaged, she'd do her best to foster the illusion. But if he didn't do something about food soon, she'd catch one of those cows she saw on the drive in and start gnawing.

"Hank Hendricks, Savannah Adams," Mike said grudgingly, glancing down at her with a frown. He'd told her not to call him Mikie.

"A pleasure, ma'am." Hank tipped his hat. "Welcome to the Bar B."

"Oh, call me Savannah. I'm practically one of the family, right?" She leaned just a bit closer to Hank, and said confidingly, "This is my first time on a ranch. Of course I'm so delighted to be here, but I have lots to learn. I'm sure you know everything."

"Yes, ma'am, uh, Savannah. I'd be pleased to show you around anytime you want." Hank smiled down at her, his eyes never leaving hers.

"I'll do the showing around," Mike ground out, not liking the way Hank looked at Savannah.

"Well, of course, *darling*, I expected you to show me around at first. But then if you get bored, I'm sure Hank can take me under his wing."

Savannah's smile was warm, almost seductive as she gazed up at Mike as if he were truly her love.

"*Darling*, as your fiancé, I can't imagine ever getting bored."

Mike turned to her and gripped her chin firmly between his thumb and forefinger. His glittering eyes warned Savannah she skated dangerously close to crossing the line.

As she held his gaze her own eyes issued their warning.

"I can guarantee you won't get bored with me, Mike Black."

She said it in the most seductive tone she could manage, while her heart rate increased fourfold and her breathing grew constricted. He captured her in the mesmerizing gaze of his dark eyes. His fingers against her skin linked them, his eyes united them, and for several seconds the rest of the world faded and there was only Mike and her, locked in a contest of wills and compelling attraction.

Desire. She'd never felt it so strongly in her life, so could be excused for being a bit slow in recognizing it. And now wasn't the time, nor was this the place, nor was Mike the man to feel it for.

Stunned that with her life totally disrupted she could spare the time to wonder if he would kiss her again like he had at the airport, her gaze never wavered. She secretly longed for another kiss. A different kind of kiss than the one from that morning. She wanted a deep, soul-shattering, toe-curling kiss that would ignite the smoldering embers of her emotions and transport her to glory.

Savannah swallowed hard. It was the strain, it had to be! Or hunger.

"Tom said you'd gotten yourself engaged, Mike.

Congratulations. What with him and Sarah tying the knot, I guess he started a trend. Conner seeing anyone?" Hank asked, oblivious to the tension shimmering between the two before him.

Mike broke away, turning to Hank. "Not that I've heard. We'll help out around here where we can, but you'll understand that we want to be alone, too."

"Sure thing. That I can understand." Hank grinned.

"We'll be down to the bunkhouse for dinner," Mike said.

"We still eat at six. See you then." Hank tipped his hat again to Savannah and headed back toward the barn.

Savannah sidestepped away, breaking contact with the disturbing marshal and drew in a deep breath in an effort to get her churning emotions under some sort of control. She wrinkled her nose.

"Yuck, what is that smell?"

Mike grinned as he reached back into the Jeep to draw out her shopping bags. "Horse, cattle, hay and a healthy dose of manure. Great, isn't it?"

Holding her breath lest she inadvertently draw in more of that great aroma, she shook her head. "I prefer salt air, thanks."

"You'll get used to it," he said unsympathetically.

Not that he'd been sympathetic about anything, she thought as she followed him into the house. At least the great aroma didn't penetrate the house, instead it smelled of lemon wax and pine cleaner.

Either Sarah had fixed up the place before they married or Mike's brother was an outstanding housekeeper. The house was immaculate.

She followed him inside the large living room. Double

pane windows framed the view of the Snowy Mountain Range. The curtains were pulled to the sides to provide a clear view. The stone fireplace on the far wall promised warmth in the cold winter months.

The furniture appeared sturdy and comfortable, with the brown and beige sofa positioned before the fireplace to offer maximum enjoyment of winter fires. The easy chairs scattered around provided places to read or watch the large screen television in the corner.

"Bedrooms are this way," Mike said, barely giving her time to scan the room before he headed down a hallway.

She followed him into a sterile room. The bed against the wall had a white spread. The white walls and white curtains were spotless, but bland. There were no pictures on the walls. A braided rag rug on the floor offered the only spot of color. That and the dark wood of the furniture.

"Guest room," he said dropping all the bags on the bed and looking around as if seeing it for the first time.

"This is nice," she said politely.

He smiled and shook his head. "I've seen motel rooms that offer more. But the bed's comfortable and I'm sure Sarah has plans once she gets back. Bathroom's two doors down on the left."

She nodded.

"My room's across the hall."

Her eyes met his. Was there a reason he told her that?

"If anything happens in the night, I'll be here in two seconds," he said, as if answering her silent question.

"But you don't expect anything to happen," she said slowly. She realized she had begun to relax for the first time in weeks.

"No, I don't. You'll be safe here, Savannah."

She nodded.

"But whether the men will or not is another story," he said, stepping closer.

"What are you talking about? Are they in danger?"

She remembered the "safe house" in Key Biscayne and how the marshal there had been injured when the living room blew up. Surely Mike didn't expect the same kind of problem here on the ranch.

"If Hank's reaction is any indication, they're all in danger. Can't you do something with your hair?"

His hands still itched to touch it, to thread his fingers through the tendrils and test how soft it was, to verify that the cloud of hair felt as silky as it looked.

"My hair?" she repeated, startled. Reaching up she gathered it to the top of her head. "Is that better?"

He swallowed hard. She'd pulled the shirt up with her arms, exposing more of that honey-tanned skin at her waist. The cotton strained across her breasts and he looked away, to be snared by the sight of the exposed nape of her neck.

What would it be like to drop a quick kiss on that honey-colored skin?

Gritting his teeth, he looked at her hair. Piled on top of her head it should have looked restrained. Instead wispy tendrils drifted down from between her fingers and skimmed her cheeks, her neck. It appeared more tantalizing than when the heavy fall hung around her shoulders.

Blast it all, he couldn't win.

"No, let it down." Pushing past her, Mike left the room.

Two seconds later, Savannah heard a door slam. Slowly she moved to the dresser and stared at her reflection. She let the hair slip through her fingers and fall back to her shoulders and below.

Maybe this attraction wasn't one-sided after all. Maybe, just maybe, Mike Black felt something when he looked at her.

She blinked and turned away. She didn't want any attraction. She didn't want anything to do with the man. Only let him keep her safe until she could return home.

Her stomach growled, reminding Savannah how hungry she was, and how long it'd been since she last ate. She walked back to the living room and found a door that led to the dining room and beyond another door led to the kitchen. Boldly opening the refrigerator, she found luncheon meat, lettuce and mayonnaise. Hunting until she found bread, she quickly made herself a huge sandwich. It'd be dinnertime soon, but she couldn't wait. This would tide her over.

As she ate, she walked around, studying the kitchen. The cabinets were of oak, the counter spacious and tiled. The stove was a bit old-fashioned, but it didn't matter to her.

She didn't like to cook. She wondered if Mike knew that. She hadn't had to cook her own meals since she'd been placed in protective custody.

And she saw no reason why that should change here. Miami had more restaurants than she could ever eat in, so meals at home had always been take out or delivered.

Tonight they'd eat with the men it sounded like. Maybe they'd take all their meals at the bunkhouse. Surely a ranch this size had its own cook.

And if not, she'd make do with sandwiches.

Picking up the second half of her sandwich, she wandered to look out the window over the sink.

She was homesick. She missed the swaying palm trees,

the salt air, and the hot sunshine. She liked the tourists that crowded Miami Beach, liked the mixed ethnic groups that offered such diversity in Miami–from old-time Southern charm to the hot-blooded Cuban influence.

Now instead of crowded streets and crowded beaches, she had endless empty rolling green hills. As she stared out the window, a kind of peace filtered in. Watching the grass moving against the wind soothed her. Almost like the mesmerizing effect of waves in the ocean. And the sky was certainly a startlingly dark blue, clear and clean. There was no pollution, no noise and no clutter.

Maybe for a vacation she could have done worse.

It was only for three weeks. She must remember that. Once the trial started, she'd be escorted back to Florida, give her testimony and then the danger would be over. Once she testified, the threat would be removed.

She hoped. No one had said what would happen if Ramirez threatened revenge.

She'd think about that if and when it happened.

In the meantime, she had three weeks of Mike Black to put up with. That presented its own danger and challenges.

If he could be trusted, she was as safe as she was ever going to be—here on his brother's ranch.

"If you're handed lemons, make lemonade," she muttered.

Maybe she could learn to ride a horse. She'd wanted a horse when she'd been a little girl. Such a long time ago. But if she learned to ride, maybe she could explore the mountains that beckoned.

"I beg your pardon?" Mike said behind her.

Turning, she colored slightly. "I talk to myself sometimes," she said, glad she'd just quoted the old cliché and not voiced the fascination she found in her host.

"Sorry I eavesdropped. I see you helped yourself to something to eat."

"Yes. You said I could eat when we got here."

"Is there enough for me?"

"Sure." She waited a heartbeat. "Want me to make you a sandwich?"

He hesitated then nodded. "Thanks, if you don't mind. I don't expect you to cook while you're here," he said, pulling out a chair and sitting at the large table pushed against the wall.

"Good, I'm not much of a cook, but I can fix sandwiches." She shrugged her shoulders. "Like everything on it?"

"The works."

He leaned back and tilted the chair on the rear legs, studying her as she drew the meat and condiments from the refrigerator.

"Why can't you cook?" he asked.

"It's not that I can't, it's that I choose not to," she replied. "When I was a teenager I earned money waiting tables. Part of the deal—free meals. I ate my way through high school and college at the Snappy Fisherman. Then when I got my job at the boutique, I started making enough money to eat out once a day. The rest I can manage."

She sliced the sandwich and looked at him. She hadn't bothered with a plate when she had her sandwich. What was she going to do with his?

He answered that when he brought the chair down on all four legs and reached for half the sandwich.

Munching on a slice of cheese, Savannah watched him eat, fascinated anew. He ate steadily, obviously as hungry as she'd been. He didn't speak, didn't try to make small talk. Feeling oddly content she let the silence stretch out.

"Let's set up some rules," Mike said as he finished the last of the sandwich some time later. "You don't wander around alone. Stick close to the house or the barn, unless you're with me. Don't answer the phone. Don't make any calls. Don't write any letters."

"Got it." It was easier than the rules at the safe house in Key Biscayne. At least here she'd have a bit more freedom.

"Keep a low profile."

"Got it."

"Savannah." He hesitated.

He wasn't sure how to say the next part, but it needed saying. Obviously her idea of a low profile and his were worlds apart.

"What?"

"Change out of Sally's jeans and into the ones you bought," he said after a silent moment.

She stared at him. "I did. These are my new ones. They're stretch jeans. I wasn't sure I would like them, but they're growing on me. They fit snugly, but look how stretchy they are."

She rose and leaned over. Keeping her knees straight, she touched her palms to the floor.

Mike about lost his teeth at the sight of her rounded bottom in the air as she demonstrated how the jeans moved with her. Had they been painted on her?

When she straightened and reached high for the ceiling, her shirt exposed that honey skin again.

He swallowed. He was going to find a pair of baggy jeans of Tom's, and a sweatshirt that'd cover her from shoulder to knees and make sure she wore them constantly!

Running in place lightly, she high-stepped to further demonstrate how comfortable the blue jeans were.

He stood and stopped her.

"They're too tight," he said.

"No, I'm telling you they're really comfortable. I didn't expect it, either, but they are!"

"They're distracting as all get out," he blurted.

She stared at him. Suddenly she stormed away, turned and glared at him.

"Don't talk to me about distracting jeans, Mr. Tight Buns. I figured you put those pants on when you were a kid and grew into them. What about the distraction you provide, huh? Am I supposed to tell you your jeans are too tight?"

He stared at her in total shock. No one had ever talked to him like that. Suddenly the humor in the situation grew too much and he chuckled.

"I'm thinking about those randy cowboys out there who'll forget how to sit a horse once they see you and you're flaring up at me."

"Let's not exaggerate here, Marshal Black."

"A low profile means keeping in the background, so people don't even notice you're around. With those jeans and that hair, there isn't a man in fifty miles who'll miss you."

All amusement faded. It'd make his job that much harder if anyone guessed who she was.

"What's wrong with my hair?"

"Nothing, only there's a lot of it and it swirls around and entices—"

He shut up. He'd said too much. Way too much. He had a job to do and by golly, he'd do it.

Her eyes narrowed and she sashayed over to him with a determination he could feel a mile away.

"There's nothing wrong with my hair or my clothes. Admit it, you don't want me here and you're stuck with me so you are trying to make me into someone I'm not."

"You got that right."

If she were dumpy, ugly and prissy he could ignore the pull of attraction that constantly shimmered barely below the surface. He was attracted to her and he didn't even know her. He'd made up his mind years ago to stay clear of involvement with women. He never forgot Amy and the havoc she'd caused.

Except for casual dates, he'd kept his vow.

But he didn't like the feelings that simmered below the surface since picking her up at the airport. Was it only a few hours ago? Or had it started when he saw her file, read about the threats and realized he could keep her safe?

He didn't know or care. He just wanted to regain his equanimity. He refused to get tangled up with some blond bombshell from Miami. He had a job to do and he would darn well do it. But if he could damp down the distractions, it'd be much easier to pull off.

Three

Savannah dressed with care for dinner. With her tan, she rarely used makeup, but did touch up her lashes with mascara and carefully applied a pink lip gloss. She fussed with her hair until it suited her, knowing it'd drive Marshal Black up the wall.

Somehow, that knowledge brightened her spirits. She had so little control over her life these days, every little bit helped.

If his expression was anything to go by when she joined him, she'd succeeded. He looked thunderous.

"I'm ready," she said brightly. It'd been two hours since she ate that sandwich and she still felt hungry.

"I could have Hank send someone over with our plates," Mike said, almost to himself.

"Oh, no, you don't. I've decided since this is likely the only time I'm going to be in Wyoming, the only time I'm going to be on a working cattle ranch, I want to see everything. And if you normally eat with the men at the bunkhouse, I want to do that, too."

"It's rough and rowdy sometimes."

"I've been places that are rough and rowdy," she countered.

She'd even lived in such places, once upon a time.

He raised an eyebrow. "Do tell."

She flushed and placed her hands on her hips, trying to look unaffected by that telling gesture. She didn't have to answer to Marshal Black, only follow his directions to keep safe.

"Try Fort Lauderdale during spring break. You won't find anything more rowdy than college kids cut loose."

He smiled, the dimple flashed. "I suspect these cowboys will give it a shot."

Just once she'd like to touch that indentation with her fingertip. Just to see how deep it went, how it felt. Blinking, she looked away.

She never wanted to do things like that. Had the mountain air addled her brains?

"Are we going or not?"

She didn't care if she sounded impatient. Maybe if she got around other people, she could get distracted from her fascination with the man in front of her.

"Yes." He ran a critical eye over her once more, sighed and moved toward the door.

By the time the heaping platters were set in the center of the long table of the communal dining room Savannah had met all the men who worked on the Bar B except for the two married ones who'd left for their own homes at the end of the workday.

The bunkhouse was unexpected. She'd envisioned it as a large single room, with bunk beds lining wooden walls and a potbellied stove in the center. The reality proved quite different.

The huge living area held sofas, tables, chairs and a large-screen television. Each man had a private bedroom, and they all shared a couple of dormitory style bathrooms. The dining room was separate, the huge industrial-size kitchen beyond.

Entering, she noticed the sign first. "No Hats, No Spurs."

Glancing around, she wondered if cowboys could read. While most of them didn't wear their hats, she heard spurs jingling as several sat down. Obviously no one paid attention to the sign. The scars on the wooden floor proved they'd ignored it for quite some time.

The chairs marched down either side of the long rectangular table, with Savannah seated smack in the center of one side. Mike sat opposite her. She tried to remember all the names as the men were introduced, but there were fourteen to dinner and she knew she wouldn't be able to keep them all straight this first night.

They were a varied bunch. Some older, one fresh from high school. Only one seemed the slightest bit overweight, the cook, Jason. The rest had a lean, whipcord physique. Similar to Mike Black, she couldn't help thinking, though a quick scan of the men convinced her none of them had the same breadth of shoulders.

Once the first pangs of hunger had been assuaged, talk around the table picked up. Everyone had a question for Savannah. How had she met Mike and convinced him to pop the question?

She smiled across the table at the marshal. "It was a whirlwind romance, wasn't it, *darling?*" she teased. "Why don't you tell them how you came to Florida and swept me off my feet?"

She threw the gauntlet down, her eyes sparkling as she

dared him. The fear of the past few months faded as she felt the security of the ranch, and the tough men who worked the place, surround her.

Mike smiled even as his eyes glittered at her challenge. "I don't have to say anything, Savannah, one look at you and every man here knows exactly how it was."

The men roared with laughter, then turned the conversation to other topics. They questioned Savannah about Miami, about the beach, the tourists, the Florida economy, and the cattle ranches in that state.

They brought Mike up to date with ranch business, told him about the changes in some of the stores or shops in town since the last time he'd visited.

Savannah talked and laughed and listened avidly. This world seemed light-years away from hers. Not one person here cared an iota about her work, despite their polite inquiries. The boutique seemed farther away than ever. Yet it had been the major part of her life for years, buying, selling, moving ahead.

In light of what happened outside the mini-mart Savannah began to question for the first time if her life contained all she wanted.

She grew quiet as she listened to the men. They fostered a feeling of family. Joking and teasing each other, the caring they shared was obvious. It wasn't something she was familiar with.

She had a few friends, but they didn't feel like family.

A career was a fine thing, but it didn't keep her warm at night,. It didn't offer her unconditional love. This situation brought it out more than ever—she was alone in the world. Not by choice, she thought darkly. First her parents had failed her. Then when she thought she'd found love—

Slowly she let her eyes rest on Mike. He laughed at something one of the men said and his expression caught her heart. He was without a doubt the best-looking man she'd ever seen. His dark hair gleamed beneath the overhead light. The planes and angles of his face were put together as if a prototype for the perfect male. Even his dimple was perfect.

Too bad his temperament couldn't be a little more even, a little more lighthearted. But when a man dealt in life and death every day, maybe lighthearted was too much to expect. She wondered why he hadn't married. It couldn't be for lack of trying on women's part. Did he consider his job too dangerous? Or had he just not found the right woman? What would she be—

"—right, Savannah?" Hank asked.

"I'm sorry, I missed that."

She dragged her gaze from Mike and looked at Hank hoping no one noticed the reason for her inattention.

"Yeah, she was gazing at Mike. They're in love," one of the other cowboys teased.

The others laughed as Savannah felt the heat climb her cheeks. She hoped that Mike thought it part of the cover, and never suspected for a single minute that she had any interest in him beyond the business at hand.

Which of course she didn't.

Precisely.

"I told the men this is your first visit on a ranch and you wanted to learn everything about it," Hank repeated, a twinkle in his eye.

"That's right." She refused to look at Mike. "Maybe I could learn to ride a horse?"

"You don't know how to ride?" one cowboy exclaimed. Wasn't he Trevor?

"I can teach you," Billy said. He looked as if he played hooky from school.

"You? Shucks, Billy, you'd put her on Wildfire. I'm much better suited to—"

"I'll teach her, of course," Mike interrupted, his eyes holding hers when she looked up.

"Now why am I not surprised?" Hank murmured, his grin big and friendly.

"Great," Savannah said, smiling with the sheer joy of the evening. "We can start tomorrow. By the time we leave, I'll be a pro."

"Mighty purty scenery to be seen around here," the older cowboy wearing the hat said.

She smiled at him and nodded. "I'd like to see as much as I can."

"If Mike gets caught up in something, give me a holler, I'll show you around," Steve said, grinning.

"In your dreams, boy," Hank said.

The men laughed again and shot a quick glance at Mike.

"This is Tom's place. I'm just here on vacation. Can't think of anything that's going to get me caught up enough to forget my fiancée," Mike said easily, his dark eyes fixed on Savannah.

It was a warning. Subtle, but effective. There was more teasing but soon everyone had enough dinner and they began to leave the table.

"Come on, darling, we'll take a quick walk around before turning in," Mike said, rising.

Savannah glanced at her watch as she rose, not even

eight o'clock. Her nap had caught her up on some of her sleep. She didn't want to go to bed too early or she'd wake up in the wee hours. What were they going to do in the meantime?

The ranch hands called good-night as she and Mike crossed the living room. Even with the door closed behind them, alone with the disapproving marshal, she felt happier than she had in a long time.

"You made a hit," Mike said, striding for the house.

"Slow down," she said, refusing to run after the man.

She'd enough running for a while. She could practically touch the house from where she stood. If he didn't want to wait for her, there was no chance of getting lost from the bunkhouse to the main house. Nor any chance of being accosted by anyone. They were alone beneath the vast evening sky.

Mike paused and turned. When she came up beside him, he reached out an arm and encircled her shoulders, encouraging her a bit to increase her pace. She shivered at his touch, alert, aware and wondering as before.

"Cold?" he asked.

She shook her head. It was cool in the early evening air. But she didn't feel the cold with his arm around her, with his body keeping pace with hers. His heat seemed to envelop her.

"We'll eat with the men to save cooking. Jason's been the cook here for a decade. Good solid food. But no more flirting," he ordered.

"Flirting? I wasn't flirting!" she said, stopping as they reached the patio beside the side door.

"Honey, you flirt like some people breathe. Maybe you

don't realize you're doing it, but when you look at a man like he's God's gift to humanity, when you smile that special smile like there's no one else in the world, when you hang on every word a man says and encourage him to say more, that's flirting in my book."

"Well, throw away your book, cowboy. I was interested in what the men had to say. This is all new to me and it's fascinating. And I was trying to be *friendly*. Smiling's a friendly thing to do. I was not flirting!"

"And I suppose the clothes you're wearing are just to be friendly?"

"My clothes? What's wrong with my clothes? Excuse me here, Mr. Marshal, but aren't you the one who made sure my only suit stayed in Denver while I was forced into cowboy attire? Aren't you the one who dragged me to a discount shopping center to buy even more cowboy outfits? And didn't every cowboy in that bunkhouse have on jeans, just like me?"

She couldn't believe they were having this conversation. She'd done nothing. Where did he come off thinking she was flirting?

Mike leaned over her until his nose almost touched hers.

"Let me tell you, sweetheart, every man in that bunkhouse may be wearing jeans, but they don't fit like yours do. They don't display hips like yours. And they sure don't wear their shirts to show any skin."

His hand covered the triangle of skin at her waist. Slowly he slipped his hand around to her back, beneath the edge of her shirt until he felt the indentation of her spine.

His voice dropped and his free hand finally gave in to the longing. He threaded his fingers through her silky hair. It felt cool and soft just as he'd imagined it.

For endless moments he gazed down into her eyes. Savannah's heart pounded and she tried to think. But it was futile. She could only feel his breath fan across her cheeks as the hard glitter in his eyes warned of his temper. Only feel the heat of his hand against her skin, or tangled in her hair.

She sighed with mingled disappointment and relief when he straightened and dropped his hands.

Already missing the contact, she wondered what it would have been like to feel his muscular body against hers. Shimmering excitement and delight splashed through her. She had never felt like this before. Not even with Robert.

The cool air struck where his warm hand had been. She shivered with the change of temperature. Glancing around, she wondered if there was any other danger on the ranch. She knew Mike Black would prove to be trouble, but it was her own reactions to his touch that'd prove the most problematic of all.

"Let's get inside," he said. In two seconds he opened the side door and flicked on an interior light.

Savannah gathered her courage and stepped into the house. She avoided his eyes, keeping her chin high. She'd done nothing wrong and certainly hadn't been flirting. Maybe she'd been a tad more exuberant in her interest around the table tonight but that didn't constitute flirting!

"We could watch some television if you like," Mike said.

"If it's all the same to you, I'd just as soon get a book or magazine and then take a bath. I've been traveling for days and would love to soak in a warm tub."

Once finished with her bath, she'd head straight for bed. Tomorrow was soon enough to face the man again.

"Oh!" She had a sudden thought.

"What?"

He quickly scanned the room, looked sharply at her. Instantly alert, his actions reminded her forcefully of their true situation.

"I forgot to get a nightgown at the store today."

Glancing down, Savannah wondered if she'd have to sleep in jeans.

"I have an old sweatshirt you can use," Mike said gruffly. "It'll cover the essentials and be warm. It gets cold here at night."

"Thank you."

Heat crept through her at the thought of wearing his shirt. It'd been next to his skin, now would be against hers. She hoped she'd sleep knowing that. First time they went into town again, she was getting her own nightie—a high-neck, long-sleeve, flannel gown!

Mike opened the refrigerator and took out a long-neck beer. Twisting off the top and tossing it into the trash, he took a long swallow of the brew before turning to head back to the living room. He wished for something stronger, but the one beer would have to do. He couldn't afford to let anything impair his reflexes or judgment.

Like almost kissing Savannah had done.

He shook his head, listening for a moment to the silence in the house. She'd gone into the bathroom a half hour ago. He'd heard the water running in the tub. Then nothing. Had she fallen asleep in the water? Had she drowned?

When he found a book for her to read and given her his

sweatshirt, she'd thanked him politely. She hadn't looked at him once since they'd left the bunkhouse—or rather since he'd held her in his arms.

Was she afraid of him?

He frowned at the thought. His job was to protect her, not come on to her. But she had nothing to worry about. He'd simply control his impulses in the future. In the meantime, however, he'd better check on her.

Walking silently down the hallway, he raised his hand to knock on the bathroom door just as it opened.

Clouds of steam billowed out. Savannah stood framed in the opening. She wore his shirt. It reached the middle of her thighs, the rest of her long tanned legs bare beneath it.

Mike swallowed, lowered his hand as his eyes caught hers, held her gaze.

"I wondered if you had fallen asleep, he said.

"No."

He stood in her way. He blocked the doorway and there was no room for her to scoot by without touching him. And he didn't think she would. He took in the folded clothes over one arm. The book with her finger between some pages.

"The book's okay?" he asked.

"It's exciting. I've never read a Louis L'Amour before. He's really good."

"I've always liked him," Mike said, leaning one arm against the jamb, forcing himself closer to her. Would she step back?

No, she tilted up her chin and met his gaze. Her eyes had curiosity blazing and for a moment Mike forgot what he was trying to do. Holding her in the yard had been a mistake. But it looked as if he might make the same mistake again.

He tightened his grip on the beer bottle, lest he toss it aside to run his fingers over the smooth line of her flushed cheeks. Her eyes were a deep blue, the sooty lashes spiked from washing her face. He wanted to run a fingertip across them, taking the water away so they fanned out like earlier.

"Uh, Mike, I need to get to bed. The air's cold on my legs," she said, licking her lower lip.

Stifling a groan, he nodded and stepped back. "Good night. Breakfast's at six-thirty."

"Six-thirty?"

She stopped and turned to look at him with a horrified expression on her face.

"The men get up early to get a start on the day. If we want to eat with them, we have to keep their hours."

"Six-thirty." She said it resignedly. "I'll be up." Sighing softly, she continued to her room and shut the door behind her.

He turned away. He had no business watching her. She'd remain in his custody until the trial. Then they'd go their separate ways. His life lay in the western states with the open spaces and cattle ranches. Hers was on the beaches of Florida.

And he'd made his decision years ago never to get involved with another woman. He'd never be burned again like he'd been with Amy.

Nor did he plan to repeat the mistakes his father made. Women and marriage and the Blacks didn't mix. Maybe his brother would prove the exception. Maybe not. But Mike had long ago made his own decision.

Heart thumping, Savannah closed her door and leaned against it for a moment. Mike had surprised her when she opened the bathroom door. Even more surprising was her own reaction. Interest was a mild term. Yet she refused to give it another name.

The coolness in the room crept beneath the fleecy shirt and she hurried to deposit her clothes on the dresser top and climb beneath the covers. The sheets were cold on her legs, but his thick sweatshirt kept her upper body warm. It wouldn't take long for her legs to warm.

She opened the book and stared at the pages. She didn't see the words, instead, she saw a tall dark man, leaning casually against the doorjamb, leaning slightly toward her. She could have reached out and touched him without moving more than an inch. Traced those firm lips, enticed by that intriguing dimple, felt the slight abrasion of his day-old beard.

She shook her head to dispel the thoughts, gripping the book tightly to banish the imagined feel of him from her fingertips.

Slowly his image faded and the words became clear. She'd read some more and then go to sleep. She ached with tiredness. Sleeping on air planes and a Jeep hadn't been very restful.

Glancing around the room, she sighed softly. For the first time in several days she felt safe. When would her life get back to normal? When would she feel safe every day?

The scream ripped through the house. In two seconds Mike burst through the door to her room, gun in hand, crouched low, alert, ready to—

She was alone. In bed. In the throes of a nightmare. The scream came again.

He swiftly crossed the room tucking the gun in the back of his waistband. He pulled her up from the pillow.

"Savannah, Savannah, wake up. You're dreaming. Wake up."

Slowly she twisted, opened her eyes. "Mike?"

"You were dreaming. You screamed so loud I thought someone had broken in and attacked you."

He sat on the edge of her bed, his hands still on her shoulders, his heart racing.

She shook her head, tears filling her eyes. "It was so awful. I hate this."

"Want to talk about it?" he asked, caressing her shoulders, kneading some of the tension away.

"It's all mixed up. The shooting I saw, the explosion at the safe house. The marshal who was cut up and bleeding from the broken glass."

She rubbed her eyes, wiped the tears from her cheeks. "The worst of it is when that man Ramirez turns to me with a gun. I try to run, but I can't go fast enough." She shuddered.

He drew her against his chest, his hands slipping down her back to soothe and comfort.

"I know it's been bad. But you're strong, Savannah Adams. You've been through a lot, more than most people, but don't let him win. You'll pull through. We're safe here. Once the trial is over, there won't be any more threats to your life. You can go home and take up where you left off."

"Maybe. Sometimes it seems as if I've been running

forever. And if I ever do get back to normal, I won't ever forget any of it."

"Maybe not totally forget. But in time the memories will fade. You'll have to really work to bring them to mind. Things will go back the way they were. The way you want things to be."

He kept his voice low, calm. His hands felt the tension seeping from her. Soon she'd be ready to drift back to sleep.

Savannah encircled his waist with her arms, holding on for dear life. She knew he'd leave soon, but for the moment it was enough he held her. It was enough that she wasn't alone. The traces of the dream gradually escaped her mind. Soon she relaxed against Mike, relishing the comfort he gave. She was so tired, yet afraid to fall back asleep. She didn't want to have that nightmare again as she had a dozen times before—it always terrified her.

Why did the night lend itself to terror? Maybe she should sleep during the day and see if the dream came as strong in the daylight. Slowly her eyes closed and she relaxed against the strength of the man holding her. She wasn't on her own for tonight.

When Savannah awoke it was still dark, but the faint tinge of pink in the eastern sky hinted at dawn. She heard a shower and turned to snuggle against her pillow.

Mike must be showering. For a moment she envisioned his sleek masculine body beneath the water, the rivulets running over his broad shoulders, across his muscular chest. Down his long legs.

Opening her eyes to stare at the dresser, she tried to control her breathing. She grew warm thinking about him. He'd been kind last night when she woke screaming.

Of course, he'd been a bit testy before that, complaining about her clothes. He was more complex than the typical cowboy image he fostered. She wondered if she'd ever feel she knew him. Would he keep himself distant while doing his job, or talk to her during the coming weeks?

Share some of himself with her while they waited together for the trial date?

She flung back the covers and, surprised at the cold, hurried to the dresser. Pulling out clean clothes, she dressed in record time. Today she tucked her shirt into the jeans, pulled her hair back into a ponytail. She felt plain. Maybe this would suit him.

She didn't analyze why she wanted to start the day without a confrontation. She'd watch to see if he was pleased to realize she followed his instructions.

She crept down the hall. The shower stopped, but she knew he was still in the bathroom, probably shaving. For a moment she considered knocking on the door just to see him. But she clamped down on that urge.

Using the second bathroom off the kitchen, she quickly washed her face and hands. When she went to the deserted living room, she crossed to the window.

The Rockies were dark, but as the sky grew lighter, their silhouette appeared against the vast horizon. Soon the sun would appear in the east and bathe the snow with all the colors of the sunrise.

"I thought you might want to sleep in," Mike said from the archway.

She turned.

He wore another blue chambray shirt, the cuffs rolled up his arms. His jeans were like the ones from yesterday, the ones that molded his legs. His hair was damp.

"Still hungry," she said, looking away.

No sense in tempting herself when her resistance was weak. This was only day two. She had weeks to get through.

He waited for her by the door and when she reached it, he tilted her chin with a finger. "No after effects of your nightmare?" he said, his eyes examining every inch of her face.

"No. I guess I fell asleep before you left?"

"You did."

"Sorry."

The dimple appeared. "No problem. I enjoyed tucking you in." He ran his gaze down her body. "It's cold outside, I've got another sweatshirt you could put on for breakfast."

"Okay."

It was cool. Later she hoped it'd warm up, but this much before dawn the mountain air was definitely chilled.

It didn't matter what she wore, he thought as they walked to the bunkhouse. Even with the shapeless sweatshirt covering her to below the sweet curve of her hips, she still looked sexy. Her hair had been drawn back into a style that should have made her look plain. But instead it emphasized her cheekbones, allowed her pretty eyes to dominate her face, made every expression chasing across evident to even the casual observer.

The men greeted her as if she were a long-time friend.

"I know Hank and Jason, Trevor and Billy and Steve." Savannah went around the table, touching each one on their shoulders. The men whose names she didn't remember reintroduced themselves. By the end of breakfast, she could attach a name to every face.

The men were charmed with her, their delight clearly evident.

Savannah joked with them and made them laugh. She asked questions and hung on every word. She tilted her head to better see them and flashed her smile.

Mike's temper grew steadily worse. She did it deliberately, he knew. He'd told her last night to stop flirting, instead she'd turned up the wattage of her smile, openly challenged his edict.

Maybe it was time she understood he wasn't playing games. This was serious. He didn't need the emotional turmoil she engendered with every man there looking at her like she had come to make his day brighter.

"Can we start riding lessons this morning?" She turned her smile on him "I'll get my hat right after we eat, then be ready. Can I learn enough to see some of the ranch if I've never ridden before?"

"We're not going riding."

Savannah blinked, her smile fading. "Why not?"

He glared at her, glanced around as the men grew silent at his brief response.

"I have a few things to check out first. Maybe later."

It wasn't a bad idea, to get her away from the other men, away from the ranch house. They could take horses, a picnic lunch and be gone all day. She'd be tired enough tonight to sleep through without waking.

First he needed to check in and verify they were in the clear.

Once assured of that, he'd find it easier to guard her with endless open range between them and danger. No one could get close to them without his seeing them long before they could prove a problem. And he knew every arroyo and canyon on the ranch. Plenty of places to hide if trouble came.

"Hank, which horse would be suitable for a first time rider?" Mike asked, touched by the excitement Savannah displayed. She really looked forward to learning to ride.

He felt a momentary pang. He hadn't planned this for her enjoyment. But it wasn't turning out that way.

He wanted to keep her away from the cowboys. She was used to being with people. Her dossier had shown him that. But her safety lay in keeping isolated, in keeping to herself and not mingling with others who could camouflage a threat until too late.

"You can take Smoky," Hank offered. "He's a fine cutting horse but gentle as a lamb. He won't give her any trouble. You'll take Tank, right? You usually ride him."

"Yeah. Smoky it is, then, thanks."

Savannah beamed at her new friend.

The men chimed in to give her advice and she tried to remember all the different bits that came fast and furiously. Finally, laughing, she admitted she'd never keep it all straight, but would do her best to stay on the horse. Her smile lit up the dining room.

Mike's scowl worsened. Breakfast was a long time ending.

Four

"I don't see why we can't go riding now," Savannah said as she watched the cowboys saddling their horses when breakfast was over. Jason remained in the bunk house to clean up after the meal.

She leaned against the fence and studied each move the men made. She could do that. The saddles looked heavy, but once she got it up on the horse, she felt sure she could tighten the strap and adjust the stirrups.

"I told you I need to check some things," Mike said evenly.

He stood far enough away that he didn't breathe her scent with every breath, yet close enough for protection if needed. He scanned the surrounding hills. A slight breeze blew from the west, cool and crisp in the early sun.

"Like?" She turned to look at him.

His eyes met hers. "Like check in with the office and get a report from my boss on what's going on. Find out if the agents in Denver saw any signs of pursuit. Once we know no one followed us, we'll take that ride. You'll be here for several weeks. Plenty of time to see the ranch."

She turned back to the corral and watched the cowboys.

Her head held high, she tried to ignore the disappointment that hit her. A few hours wouldn't make a difference. They'd ride later, once he knew she was safe.

"Come back to the house with me." Mike touched her shoulder.

She tried to ignore the shimmer of sensation that splashed through her at his touch, but she couldn't. Glancing up at him, she saw no sign of a reciprocal awareness.

He was doing his job—protecting her. There was nothing more to their relationship. Savannah wondered if she should be more proactive as his fiancée. Maybe they should hold hands, flirt a bit. Just for the other cowboy's sake, of course.

She smiled, imagining Mike's reaction if she suggested such behavior.

Once inside, Savannah looked at Mike. "Now what?"

"I need to wait before calling in, no one'll be in the office yet. Why don't you do whatever it is you do at home?"

"At home, as you put it, I'm usually at work by now. I'd be reviewing sales results, planning new marketing strategies, making arrangements for a fall showing, and—"

His finger on her lips stopped her. She blinked.

"What about the weekends? What do you do at home on the weekends?" he asked softly.

Jerking her head away Savannah took a step backward. Her lips tingled where he'd touched. Frowning, she looked away. She didn't like this attraction. For years she had been her own boss, answering to no one, not even her own emotions. She had made her life the way she wanted it.

"Many weekends I go into work. The shop's open seven days a week because of the tourist crowd. We get a lot of business on the weekends."

He took off his hat and tossed it on the nearest table.

"You must do something for relaxation. Maybe paint your fingernails?"

Her eyebrows rose in disbelief. She held out her hands, the nails short and covered in clear polish.

"Heck, I don't know. Go fix your hair. That should take an hour."

Narrowing her gaze, she glared at him. "I pulled it into a ponytail because you warned me not to look glamorous, now you want me to go *fix my hair*? Can we have a little consistency here, Marshal?"

"You asked me what you could do, I was coming up with ideas!"

"Fine." She snatched off the rubber band, dropped it on the floor and ran her fingers through her hair, tousling it with her hands. "How's that?" she dared, her fists on her hips.

Mike almost groaned aloud. She looked gorgeous. Her hair floated about her face and shoulders like a golden cloud. It looked as fine as silk. He wanted to touch it again, feel the softness cling to his fingers. Have tendrils curl around him as if she were drawing him in closer.

"I don't care what you do. I'm here to guard your life, not entertain you. Go stare out the window for all I care. Only don't leave the house unless I'm with you."

With that he stormed down the hall, his boots loud on the polished wooden floor. The temptation to slam the door to his brother's office was almost more than he could resist. But resist he did.

Crossing to the desk, he sank down hard and glared at the phone. He'd call his boss at home. He didn't want to wait until after nine to get in touch at the office. The sooner he knew they were in the clear, the sooner he could get away from the house and gain some perspective.

Savannah stared down the hall, wishing he'd come back so she could tell him exactly what she thought of his nasty comment. She didn't need anyone to entertain her. She'd been on her own for years, she could take care of herself. And so she'd tell the man if he ever said anything like that again.

Turning, she crossed the room to the window. Slowly she pulled back the sheer curtain that hampered her view. At the safe house in Florida she hadn't been allowed near the windows for safety reasons. Here she had more freedom than in the last few months. But she still felt like a prisoner. And Mike was nothing more than her jailer.

So why did she feel so attracted to him? Why did her heart pound when he drew near? And why did she long for another kiss? The man had no interest in her beyond his job.

He thought she was frivolous. *Go fix your hair. That should take an hour.* As if that would satisfy her. Did he think she was so shallow?

Tempted to prove that she was not, she glared outside, her mind spinning with ideas. But after a moment she leaned her forehead against the cool glass, her need for revenge fading.

He was right. She had to find patience somewhere to wait out the last three weeks.

Mike wasn't her jailer, only the man trying to keep her alive until she could testify. He was willing to put his life on the line for hers, just like the other marshals. Justice would be served if she could make it to the trial and testify. That was paramount.

Fine. She'd make sure she kept her mind on the business at hand. Somehow she needed to get through the next three weeks. Then life as she knew it would return to normal.

Only—it wouldn't be the same. She'd changed over the last six months. Would her former lifestyle be enough?

The thought startled her, frightened her. It had to be, there was nothing else for her.

Letting the curtain drop, Savannah walked back to her room and picked up the book she started last night. Flopping on the bed, she punched the pillows up behind her head and began to read. Before long her eyes drifted closed and she slept.

"Savannah?" Mike shook her gently.

"What?" Slowly she came awake, gazed up at the man leaning over her bed. "What?"

"Do you still want to go riding?" he asked, amusement lurking in his eyes.

"Yes." She pushed the book away and sat up. Mike stood only inches away. Would he move when she stood? The backs of his fingers caressed her cheek.

"You have a crease mark."

She stood up, disappointed when he stepped back.

"I didn't mean to fall asleep. What time is it?"

"Just after ten. Have you been asleep all this time?"

"I guess. I tried to read but couldn't stay awake—probably jet lag."

She moved to the chest of drawers and took her brush. Pulling it through her hair, she met his eyes in the small mirror situated on top of the chest.

"Leave you hair down if you like. It will only be you and me this afternoon. I got a picnic lunch from Jason."

"Why, Marshal, how special. And I thought you weren't going to entertain me," she said pertly.

His eyes narrowed at her tone. "We can stay home," he threatened.

She turned. "No. I want to go."

He left the room and walked out to the living room. Savannah caught up her new hat, plopped it on her head and hurried after him, afraid he might change his mind.

In less than twenty minutes Savannah and Mike were mounted and riding out of the barnyard. Savannah had never ridden before and the horse seemed enormous when she first stood beside him. Trevor saddled both horses and had them ready for them when they left the house.

Eyeing the stirrup, she wondered how she would ever get up on his back. The way became clear when Trevor cupped his hands together for her to step into. Savannah settled into the saddle and glanced at Mike. Already mounted, he watched her, his expression thoughtful.

Now what? she thought. Trying to ignore the bubbling of excitement in her chest, she held the reins as Trevor showed her and nodded her understanding to his brief commands. He double checked that her stirrups were at the right length for her.

"Take it easy," Trevor said, smiling up at her, his expression friendly.

"I'm not going anywhere a beginner can't go," Mike replied gruffly. He urged his horse forward and Savannah's gelding stepped in behind.

The rhythm of the horse's gait was soothing and in only a few moments she forgot about being nervous and began to relax and take notice of her surroundings.

They moved slowly away from the homestead, onto the grassy range that appeared to stretch out forever. The sun shone warm and bright. She reached up and pulled her hat down over her forehead enough to shelter her eyes. Looking around with excitement, she forgot that only yesterday she'd wanted to go to Southern California. Today was perfect.

She'd yearned for a horse as a child, and now she was riding! Gingerly, she reached out and patted his neck.

Mike sat tall in the saddle and never looked back to see if she followed. Maybe he could hear her horse. But she wished he'd at least glanced around toward her once to make sure she hadn't fallen off. He seemed to have time to look everywhere else.

"Are we in danger here?" she called, bravely kicking her horse to get him to catch up with Mike's.

He drew rein and waited for her to come alongside him. "I wouldn't have suggested the ride if I felt there was any danger. I checked with my boss earlier. All indications are those in pursuit lost you. No one followed us here, no one suspects you're here."

"You say that with a lot of assurance," she murmured, looking around at the vast empty plains.

"Another safe house in Florida was hit last night. It was empty this time, but we think whoever is after you believes you're still in Florida."

"Another bomb?" she asked, shivering slightly at the memory of the last attack.

"Yes. No one hurt, but it points out the possibility of a leak in the regional office."

"So your plan's working."

She smiled at him, hoping he'd take the olive branch. If

she were stuck in the middle of a Wyoming ranch, she at least wished her companion was—well, companionable. Mike treated her like she was—a job. Which she was.

And she didn't need any special treatment. Only... only she wished he could be as friendly as the cowboys who worked on the ranch.

She remembered his kiss at the airport.

This morning he treated her as if she had the plague.

He stared at her long and hard. Savannah began to fidget in the saddle, her horse sidestepping away.

"I'm glad to get the chance to ride. Did I tell you when I was a kid, I always wanted a pony?" She'd try for normalcy. If he didn't respond, she'd try something else.

"And did you get one?" he asked.

She shook her head and looked away.

"No. We didn't have much money. I was lucky to get new shoes for school each year. There was no way I'd ever have a horse. But I sure wanted one."

For a moment she remembered the little girl who had been so horse crazy.

Then realization set in and she ducked her head until the brim of her hat hid her face from Mike. How could she have mentioned the bit about shoes? She'd long moved beyond her past.

She had money enough now to afford a new pair of shoes every week if she wanted them. The poor little girl she'd once been was gone and she didn't want to remember those days.

"Tough. But the flip side of that is if you had horses, you'd have spent a lot of time mucking out stables, soaping your leather and exercising the horse."

"I guess." She watched the grass ripple in the breeze. "The riding would have been fun, I think."

"Now is as good a time as any, I guess," Mike said.

"For what?" She looked around and met his gaze. How could any man have such long eyelashes? It wasn't fair. Her own lashes were thick and curled slightly, but they were not as long as his. For a moment she didn't register what he said.

"We've got three weeks ahead of us. I told you last night to quit flirting with the men. This morning I might as well have held my breath. We need to get some things clear."

"I was not flirting," she said through gritted teeth. "Marshal, in case you've forgotten, you brought me here. You're the one who proposed the fake engagement. I'm merely trying to play a part. What would you have me do, ignore their overtures? Snub every last one of them? Would that be in keeping with a woman you'd get tangled up with? I thought I played my part well. You should be thanking me, not yelling."

For a moment Mike was silent, remembering Amy. He'd never brought her to the ranch, because he hadn't wanted to share her with anyone. How would Amy have acted if he'd brought her home?

His eyes narrowed while he studied the young woman beside him trying to manage her horse. Savannah was correct, she hadn't asked to be assigned to him, but she was his responsibility. He came up with the ploy to keep the ranch hands from questioning why he was here. If there was to be any gossip around town, it'd be the seven day wonder of his becoming engaged. No one would suspect he was guarding a valuable witness.

"If we were really engaged, you'd flirt with me. That

would be playing your part," he said slowly, wondering if he were acting like an idiot suggesting she flirt with him. Was he any less susceptible than the men who worked the Bar B?

"If I decide to flirt, Marshal, you'll be the first to know," she said sassily. "In the meantime, are you going to show me this ranch or shall I just learn to sit on a restless horse? Something tells me my legs are going to regret this tomorrow."

Mike smiled. "Sooner than that. Probably before you go to sleep tonight."

"Great, another thing to look forward to. You don't have to look so cheerful about it. Where are all the cattle we saw yesterday when we drove in?"

He nudged his horse and headed up a slight rise. "Come on and I'll show you."

Savannah quickly caught up, pleased with herself for remembering Trevor's instructions. And more pleased that the horse seemed to remember them, as well.

"Forget your troubles, Miss Adams, and enjoy the best that Wyoming has to offer."

"Not easy to forget. But I'm looking forward to learning a bit about this place. I doubt I'll be back."

"No, I don't suppose you will."

"So, Marshal, tell me how a Wyoming cowboy became a law enforcement officer. Was it the glamour of wearing a badge?"

He shook his head. "Not the badge—the glamour of the job."

She laughed, feeling free for the first time in months. "Right. It's so glamorous, dodging crooks in back corridors of airports, hiding in safe houses that aren't safe, baby-sitting people on cattle ranches."

"There is a bit more to it than that," he drawled.

"Most of it dangerous, I suspect."

She remembered the deputy who had been injured in the safe house.

"Sometimes, but mostly it's routine, like any law enforcement agency. Why did you become a boutique manager? For the glamour?"

"You're darn right. Only it turns out to be a lot more work than glamour. But I do get a discount off my clothes. That helps."

That was at the beginning. At first she wanted to have nice clothes and found the boutique the perfect answer.

But once she began working, she soon wanted to move up in the business. Wanted to be in charge of making decisions, seeing if her ideas would work. In a relatively short time she'd moved up to supervisor then manager. Now the entire operation was managed between her and Paulette Stevens, the owner. And she had a shot of buying into the business.

Unless Paulette had changed her mind during her long absence.

"I bet your boutique doesn't even carry jeans," he teased.

"We do, too. Only they are not the kind you'd want to ride a horse on. They cost too much for one thing. But I'm not sure they're as comfortable as these."

She threw him a glance from beneath the brim of her hat. They'd been talking casually for several minutes. Surely a record.

"There're the cattle you asked about." He pulled to a stop at the summit of the hill. Below them spread out over several acres grazed the white faced cattle she'd glimpsed yesterday.

Pulling her horse to a stop, Savannah gazed down at the sight. "Wow, a million hamburgers on the hoof. Are they dangerous?"

"Not particularly. Want to ride down among them?"

She hesitated, then shook her head. "Not today, at any rate. I think I'm doing fine to be staying on the horse."

He chuckled. "Sitting on a horse while he plods along almost doesn't count as riding."

"Well, it suits me just fine."

"Then let's head this way and I'll show you the river."

He turned his horse to the left and ambled along the ridge, then heading down the hill toward a bank of trees. His eyes constantly scanned the area, searching for anything out of place.

Savannah followed, wishing she knew the man better. He certainly wasn't the talkative type. She wondered if that was part of his personality or his duty while she remained in his custody.

"Ever been married, Marshal?" she asked daringly, hoping to jar him into some response.

"Never." His reply was clipped.

Curiosity piqued, she tried to analyze his answer. His face remained impassive, his eyes focused on the trees in the distance. Sounded like not only never, but never would be.

"Me, either," she said a moment later, wishing he had at least asked.

"Come close?" he asked, skirting a small cluster of rocks and easing his mount down a slight incline.

Savannah didn't know whether to reply or not.

"Savannah?" His voice sounded gentle. His eyes met hers, the curiosity blatant.

She looked at him and shrugged. "Once, a long time ago."

"Your dossier didn't mention any man," he said thoughtfully.

"My dossier?" She yelled the words. "You have a dossier on me?"

"The office does. We got it sent by courier when we knew we'd be handling the case. It's routine."

"I can't believe it. How detailed is it? How dare you read a dossier on me! Good grief, I don't want my life splattered all around for everyone and his brother to see."

"My brother didn't see it," he replied, his lips twitching.

She only glared at him. "I don't find that funny. So you know everything there is to know about me and I know nothing about you." Her eyes narrowed "Just how much do you know?"

"We know your background from schooling, where you work, where you live. Lighten up, Savannah, it's part of the job."

"I'm sick of hearing about the job."

She yanked on the reins and her horse stopped so suddenly she lost her balance. Scrambling to keep from failing off, she grabbed the saddle horn as she watched Mike stop and turn back to her.

"Problem?"

"If you know so much about me, I think it only fair I should know something about you. If I were to hire a bodyguard, I'd sure check him out before taking him on."

"Seems reasonable. What do you want to know?" His

eyes studied her.

She hesitated, she wanted to know everything! But that was over the top and unnecessary. Soon she'd return to Miami and never set eyes on this man again.

"Did you come close?" she asked, wondering why she concentrated on that one aspect of the man's life.

"To what?"

"To getting married."

He hesitated. While his eyes seemed steady on hers, he seemed to look back a long way.

Savannah regretted asking as soon as the words were out of her mouth, but she wouldn't back down.

And she found it very interesting that he hesitated so long. There was something in his background that—

"I thought about it once," he admitted slowly. His gaze focused in on her, direct and clear. "But it didn't work out. What happened with you?"

"I thought I was asking the questions. You already know about me."

"Not about almost getting married. That wasn't in the file."

She drew in a deep breath, looked away from his penetrating gaze. "I-it was when I was in college. I had to work my way through. But I'm sure you know all that. Anyway, Robert Hanson was a pre-med student. We met, started dating."

For a moment the memories flooded. She'd refused to dwell on them for years. It surprised her how fresh and clear they appeared. And that they could still bring an ache to her heart.

"Anyway, I misread the situation. He wasn't interested

in marriage."

"Why does that sound like an abbreviated version?" Mike asked, shifting in his saddle as his horse leaned down to graze on the green grass.

"It's enough. Your turn."

He hesitated a moment, then seemed to make up his mind. "I fell for a woman in Denver. We were in love. Or so she led me to believe. Only it was just a setup. She wanted more than I could give her. When I didn't leave the marshal's service to join her daddy's electronics firm, our relationship ended. I don't plan to make another mistake like that."

"Like believing in love or falling for someone who wants you to change?" Savannah asked.

"Either. Do you want to see the river or not?"

"Yes."

They rode in silence until they reached the banks of the Laramie River. Mike dismounted and turned to help Savannah. She shook her head.

"I can manage."

It wasn't graceful, but manage she did, landing with a jar. Her legs felt like cooked spaghetti. She stomped her feet to get the circulation moving and walked to the water's edge, her horse following docilely at her side.

"This is beautiful," she said slowly, delighting in the beauty of the setting.

"I thought we'd eat lunch here," Mike said.

"Nice."

Her horse nudged against her as he passed her. His front hooves splashed when he waded in and lowered his head to drink. She clung to the reins, but gave him enough leeway to enable her to stay on dry land.

Savannah thought about their recent conversation as she watched the horse drink. Both had been burned in love. Both were too wary to succumb again. Maybe they could be friends of a sort for the next few weeks or maybe not. At least there'd be no danger of stronger emotions. They were immune.

For a moment she wondered if that was a good thing. Then decided it was. The physical attraction would fade once they'd been around each other for a while. Nothing here would remind her of the heartbreak she'd once experienced.

"What do we do with the horses while we eat?" she asked.

"We'll let them drink their fill, then ground hitch them over in that grassy area. They'll eat while we eat."

It was pleasant beside the river, the cottonwoods that lined the banks shaded the ground, the breeze blew fresh and cool across the water. Savannah watched mesmerized as the river flowed south, wishing it was warm enough to go swimming. She missed the beach, missed the water.

The day was proving to be a treat. She'd been confined to the safe houses in Florida far too long. No walks along the beach. No sitting in the backyard for the sun.

Mike settled both horses in a patch of lush grass in the sunshine. He pulled the saddle bags from his and went back near the river, sitting on the sparse grass in the shade.

"No blanket?" Savannah asked, sitting beside him after first looking for something a little cleaner than grass and dirt.

"Nope."

"The good thing about jeans, huh? You can sit anywhere."

"Right. Here, two sandwiches are for you. I had Jason

pack two each, I know your appetite," he said sitting handing her two wrapped sandwiches.

"I really don't have that big an appetite. I just hadn't eaten in a long time yesterday."

Her first bite changed her mind. Maybe she would eat both, they were delicious. Or was it being outdoors? Or being with Mike Black? Whatever, she'd make the most of the day.

Savannah proved Mike correct. She ate all her lunch, two sandwiches, three chocolate chip cookies and an apple. Sitting quietly beside the flowing river, she let its soft murmur soothe her. In the shade with the light breeze Savannah was comfortable. Maybe summer in Wyoming wasn't so bad after all.

"I wish we could go swimming," she said wistfully.

He leaned back, resting his head on his saddlebags, tilting his hat over his face. "Go ahead. I'm going to take a nap. Someone woke me up last night and I had a hard time going back to sleep."

She flushed, remembering her nightmare.

"I didn't bring a bathing suit," she replied primly.

"Strip down to your undies and go for it. There's only you and me out here."

"Right."

She frowned. It was tempting. She knew she had a good figure and if she were confident enough, she wouldn't mind swimming in underwear, her panties and bra would cover as much as her bikini.

But she couldn't do it. Not with sexy Mike Black reclining a few yards from the water. She'd know it was underwear and not a proper swimsuit. That was a bit too much.

He lifted his hat an inch and looked at her. "Can't you swim?"

Nodding, she turned. "Of course I can. But if you think I'm going to take off my clothes for you—"

"Not for me, Ms. Adams. I told you, I'm not interested."

She took a deep breath and turned back to the river. How clear could the man make it? Even if she took off her clothes, he wasn't the least bit interested. She risked a glance over her shoulder. His hat was back in place, his hands folded across his chest. His breath slow and even. Had he fallen asleep so quickly?

She pulled off her boots, then her socks. Maybe she wouldn't go swimming, but she could wade in the cool water. It'd be better than sitting on the grassy bank waiting for her guard to waken.

She rolled up her pant legs, stood up and dusted off her bottom. Walking to the river, she smiled. It was almost as good as being at the beach with the added bonus of no crowds.

Her shriek brought Mike up in one smooth movement. In less than a second he stood beside her, by the water's edge, searching the trees and range as if he'd throw his body between hers and danger, gun in hand.

"What's wrong? Did you see someone?" he asked.

"What's wrong? *That water is freezing!* I almost went swimming in it!"

Slowly he stood up to his full height. "You screamed like you were being killed over a little cold water?"

"A little cold? That water feels like ice! I'm lucky I don't have frostbite on my toes."

He smiled. "The water's snow melt, it's always cold, except in late summer in some of the shallow areas."

"You could have warned me."

Incensed at his amusement, she pushed against him. It threw him off balance. As he went down, his hands caught hers and pulled her with him. The splash almost reached his saddlebags.

"Aaiiieee! Get me out of here, this water's freezing!"

Savannah pushed against him and tried to get her feet beneath her. The water flowed around them, taking them a few feet downstream from their picnic site. Her breath caught, she could hardly breathe for the cold. Icy moisture found every inch of her body, soaking her clothes and her hair.

Mike stood up laughing. He shook his head, water flying.

"I thought you said you could swim," he teased, and reached for her hand drawing her to her feet.

"Of course I can." She pulled away and stomped to shore, only a few feet away. Once she had her feet firmly on dry ground, Savannah scurried up to the sun. Her hair hung down her back, water streamed off her. She turned back to the river. "Oh, my new hat." The once-white hat floated on the water, near Mike's darker one, both almost out of reach.

Mike pushed against the bottom, swam two strokes and snatched up both hats. He turned and began making his way to the shore. The water hit him mid-chest. And he still chuckled.

Savannah shivered in the light breeze, hoping the sun's warmth would soon take the edge off being so cold. She was used to warm seas not freezing mountain rivers.

And if he didn't stop laughing, she'd push him back in again. Only this time stay well clear of his hands!

Coming from the river, Mike followed her into the sunshine.

"It's not funny. I didn't dodge bullets in Florida just to freeze to death in some Wyoming river," she snapped, wringing the water from her long hair. Her clothes clung to her like a second skin. She peeled her shirt from her breasts and held it away from her for a semblance of modesty. The sunshine and breeze would probably dry her before long, if she didn't freeze to death first.

"You couldn't freeze to death in that short time. The water's cold, but not life threatening. We swam in it all the time as kids."

"Well, I'm not a kid and I'm used to warm water."

He let his gaze roam over her figure, every square inch now clearly defined by the wet shirt and jeans. His laughter eased when she saw she was shivering.

Without thinking, Mike dropped their hats and reached for her, drawing her up against his hot body.

"Does this help?" he asked, wrapping his arms around her and molding her sexy figure against his frame. It sure warmed him up.

Savannah stopped shivering and wrapped her arms around the solid man standing against her. His body felt like a furnace, warming her instantly. More than warming her, starting a conflagration within. She tried to resist, but the heat that licked through her veins wouldn't be denied. Slowly she raised her face until her eyes met his. Before she could say a word, his face blocked the sun and he covered her lips with his own.

Five

"Blast it!" Mike pushed Savannah away. "I swore I wouldn't do that again!"

She shrugged out from under his grip and turned lest he see the flaming color in her cheeks.

"Consider it first aid, Marshal. I was cold, you warmed me up."

Oh wow, had he warmed her up. She bit her lower lip. She hadn't meant to confess that, she needed to maintain her cool. The last thing she wanted was for him to suspect how much his kisses affected her. Someone needed to keep a level head and it'd better be her.

His finger came beneath her chin, tilting her head around until she had to look at him. Slowly his thumb brushed across her lips, as if fascinated by the texture of her skin.

"We need to get home and change. Are you all right?"

"Unless you count freezing cold. Remind me not to mention swimming again any time soon."

She tilted her chin and bravely met his gaze, hoping desperately that the confusion and longing tangled within her didn't show to this astute law officer.

"Hey, you pushed me," he protested, amusement dancing in his eyes.

"Believe me, I'm sorry now." In spite of being wet and cold, the humor of the situation finally hit her and she grinned. "You could have warned me."

"At least you had the sense to go in without your boots. Mine are full of water."

She giggled at that. "Better empty them out or you'll have extra weight on your horse."

He nodded, brushed his thumb over her lips once more and turned away. Sitting on a dry patch of ground, Mike pulled off his boots. Trickles of water poured out onto the dirt, which instantly turned to mud. He took off his socks and wrung them out before pulling them back on. Stomping into his boots, he grimaced. "Not the most comfortable feeling."

Savannah watched him as she wrung out the tails of her shirt, skimming her palms against the denim, trying to get rid of some of the water. When she looked up again, she caught her breath. Mike had taken off his shirt and was in the process of wringing water from it.

His chest muscular, his skin a warm teak.

She stopped dead and stared, feeling the now familiar heat licking deep within. Knowing she had to look away, she delayed, tantalized beyond belief by the sheer male perfection of the man. She wished she dare trace those muscles with her fingertips, run a fingernail across the washboard stomach, taste the bronzed skin.

When he shook out the shirt, she raised her eyes and met his hot gaze. For a moment, time stood still. Then Savannah drew in a ragged breath.

"I'll turn around and you can take off your shirt and wring it out," Mike said, his voice husky. Did he feel it, too, the wanting, the desire?

She nodded, her eyes dropping back to that broad expanse of male chest. When he turned, she stared at his back just as tanned, just as muscular. How did he keep so fit? Did he exercise? Or was it from his work on the ranch?

"Savannah?"

She jumped. "What?"

"Are you almost finished?"

She hadn't even started. "Almost. I'll tell you when to turn around."

Unfastening her shirt she peeled it off her skin. The warmth of the sun hit instantly. Slowly she twisted the cotton until she couldn't get any more water out of it. She snapped it in the air to shake out the wrinkles.

Mike turned at the sound and stopped.

"I said I'd tell you when," she said, clutching the damp shirt against her breasts.

Her bra was wet and almost transparent. She swallowed, heat engulfing her from the inside out. Maybe she should plunge back into the river to cool down.

"I didn't know what made that sound. It's my job to watch out for you."

"That's watch out for, Marshal, not watch."

She was female enough to recognize the flare of interest in his eyes, woman enough to be pleased, innocent enough to be uncertain.

He smiled and shook his head. "Right, Ms. Adams, but I do take my job seriously."

She spun around and struggled into her wet shirt. Buttoning it up, she turned back, disappointed to find Mike had donned his own shirt. Only he'd left it unbuttoned, which revealed tantalizing glimpses of his chest. Savannah took a shaky breath. She glanced at her shirt, halfway expecting it to be steaming from the heat that rushed through her. It clung to her skin, to every curve and indentation. If she had a blanket she's wear it like a shawl. Brazening it out, she lifted her chin and met his eyes in a bold challenge.

"I'll get my boots," she said, then spoiled her act by rushing past as if she were in a race. A race to keep her heart and mind intact.

The ride back proved uncomfortable. Wet jeans chafed. The wind picked up causing shivers as it danced against the damp material. The sun played peek-a-boo with fluffy white clouds causing Savannah to feel more miserable than she'd felt in ages. When the ranch house came into view, she was delighted. A hot bath and dry clothes sounded like heaven.

"Can't we go faster?" she asked, wishing she felt comfortable on a horse to ride hell-for-leather. But today was her first venture and she was not that brave.

"Not this close to the barn. We need to make sure the horses don't run the last bit," Mike said, glancing over at her. "And are you ready for a faster gait?"

"I can't wait until I get into a hot bath," she murmured, silently urging her horse to go faster. She'd hang on, no matter what.

"Once we see to the horses you can have the bathroom first."

"See to the horses? What's to see to?"

Dismayed, she looked at Mike. Was he serious?

Mike glanced around the yard as they rode in. "The men are out working. Someone needs to take these saddles off and brush the horses, pick the hooves. Did you think that work got done by elves?"

She bit back the reply that sprang to mind.

"Look on it as finally getting your wish," he said as he stopped his horse and easily dismounted. Leading the gelding into the dark barn, he left Savannah to fend for herself.

She threw her leg over the saddle and almost fell to the ground. Clinging to the saddle horn until her legs were strong enough to support her, she followed Mike into the barn, Smoky trailing behind her, his reins in her hand.

In her next childhood, she'd wish for a hot tub.

"I don't know the first thing about taking care of horses," she said.

"You'll never learn any younger."

"I thought you were to guard me, not teach me ranching," she grumbled.

Cold, wet and miserable didn't induce good moods.

"Where I come from everyone pulls his, or her, own weight," he said.

"And you're suggesting I don't?" Anger began to lick around the edges.

Mike lifted the saddle from his horse and tossed it on a wooden frame. He looked at Savannah.

"I don't know what you do, Savannah. Do you pull your own weight? Or do you want someone to wait on you? I've known you for a day."

A day? Was that all? It seemed longer.

She tied her horse where Mike indicated and began to unfasten the saddle, struggling to get the leather strap out of the cinch.

"I thought you knew all about me from my dossier," she

mumbled, unwilling to let the silence build.

"I know facts but nothing about the woman they represent."

She pulled the saddle off and promptly fell backward, sitting down hard on the packed ground. The saddle must weigh seventy-five pounds!

Mike lifted it easily and placed it beside his saddle. Offering a hand to help her up, he said nothing, just watched her from eyes that gave nothing away.

She ignored his hand and scrambled to her feet unaided. Brushing off her damp jeans, she began unbuckling the bridle. Mike's hand covered hers. "Wait until we take the horse to the corral before you take off the bridle. Then you can just turn him loose."

She nodded, slipping her hands free. The tingles that shimmered up her arms at his touch did nothing to ease her frustration and uncertainty. She wanted to finish and escape. She needed time to think and she couldn't do it around him—she was too caught up in the roiling sensations that filled her any time he came near.

It took forever. She brushed the horse, but missed spots, which Mike quickly pointed out. She learned to pick the hooves and comb the mane and tail. Finally she satisfied the man and turned the horse loose in the corral.

"Good job," Mike said as they walked back to the house.

Unbidden, a warm glow of satisfaction flooded Savannah. It'd been a long time since anyone had complimented her on a job well done. She tilted her head back and smiled up at the man.

"Thank you, Marshal. Have you thought you missed a great career by not being in the military? You seem to love to give orders."

He stopped and encircled her neck with one hand, pulling her around before him. "In the military the subordinates don't talk back."

"Maybe I don't feel subordinate," she sassed, tingling from his touch.

Warm bath forgotten, excitement filled her. It was dangerous trading words with the man, but a danger she felt up to meeting.

"Probably not. You're far too cocky."

She could feel every finger where he held her. She didn't move, wanting to step closer, knowing that was the dumbest thing she could do. Physically attracted to the man, she wasn't sure she liked him. Her track record with the opposite sex wasn't very good. Distance was what she needed more than anything. Distance and perspective.

"Stop flirting and go take your bath," he said, giving her neck a gentle squeeze and releasing her.

"I was *not* flirting!"

"If that smile isn't designed to have men sink to their knees, I'd like to see one that is."

She smiled brightly, for once trying her wings at flirting just to get his goat. She lightly brushed his chest, letting her fingers soak in the heat from his hot skin. She dare not do more, but it was tempting, oh, so tempting.

"Take your bath!" he ground out.

"Another order, Marshal?" she asked, widening her eyes slightly, deliberately licking her lips to moisten them.

Staring at her mouth, he nodded slowly. "More back talk, Ms. Adams?"

"Just clarifying things," she drawled, looking up at him

from beneath her lashes. Her smile grew smug as his expression grew grim. "Lighten up, Marshal."

"That can get someone killed," he said.

Savannah sighed and turned toward the house. His comment killed the fun. She was damp and cold, her hair a mass of windblown tangles. Her new hat stained and drooping. The ride had started so promising and ended with regret.

She wished she were home. She missed the life she'd built for herself. She was as out of place on this working cattle ranch as she'd have been skiing in the Olympics. The sooner she got back to Florida, the better.

Savannah took a hot bath, then went to her room. She dressed warmly in clean jeans and a long-sleeve shirt. She had to do laundry soon, the few things she'd bought didn't cover being drawn into a creek. Taking her book, she lay on the bed, her eyes scanning the words, her mind replaying their ride.

Several hours later her stomach began to growl. She closed the book and sighed. Checking the time, she wondered why Mike hadn't called her for dinner. Surely it had to be time to eat, she was starving. She brushed her hair and opened the door to her room.

Mike sat on the sofa in the living room, the various sections of a newspaper tossed haphazardly around him as he finished reading the last section.

"Isn't it time for dinner?" Savannah asked, pausing in the doorway.

"Jason's bringing it over for us tonight," he replied, without looking up.

She wandered over to the window. "Why?"

Pulling back the sheer curtains, she looked at the bunkhouse. No sign of anyone. Maybe she should fix a sandwich to tide her over.

He lowered the paper and looked at her. "I told him we wanted to be alone tonight."

She frowned, still staring out the window. "Why? We've been together most of the day. Wouldn't you like a bit of a break?"

"I spent part of the afternoon working on the tack in the barn. I assume you didn't see my note since it was where I left it when I returned."

"I didn't miss you," she said caustically.

She sighed and turned back to the room, plopping down in a chair that faced the sofa.

He looked at her. "Did you get all dressed up on my account?" he asked.

She blinked. "What are you talking about? These are just jeans."

"Your hair and all that makeup."

"I think you have a fixation on my hair, Marshal. I brushed it after I washed it this afternoon. It's naturally wavy, I didn't do anything special. And I don't have any makeup. You didn't give me time enough in that store to buy any. All I have is a mascara wand in my purse."

"You look like you have on blush."

"Sun."

"What?"

"It's from the sun. I've been cooped up for so long, all my tan's faded. Can you imagine how hard it was confined to a house in Miami? The weather's been beautiful all spring, and I was stuck behind closed doors. Being in the sun today turned my skin pink."

"We'll try to get out more," he said gently.

"You said this place is safe. Can't I go outside on my own, if I stay close to the house or barn?"

Mike hesitated. So far there was no evidence that they'd been followed. In fact the break-in at the second safe house gave him reason to believe the men after Savannah still believed she was in Florida. It was his job to protect her. However, maybe he could let one or two of the trusted cowboys know why they were here. They could watch out for her if he wasn't with her.

"My job's to keep you safe."

"Great, but don't make me a prisoner. Darn it, I didn't do anything but be in the wrong place at the wrong time. Ever since the attacks on my life, I've been kept locked up to keep me safe. Before that, my life was threatened twice. And I actually escaped an attack. I'm used to being with people, used to doing things, building a career, visiting with friends. I hate this."

"Stay close to the house or the barn. Don't go anywhere else. And if you see anything that looks suspicious, find me," he said at last.

Savannah's eyes lit up as she smiled. "Thanks! That'll help. Maybe tomorrow I'll lie in the sun for a while and work on my tan."

Mike snapped the paper up before him, but didn't see the newsprint. He imagined Savannah's hair in the sun, all golden and bright like the sun itself. He knew her skin would deepen that honey tan in another day or two, the blush of sunburn changed. But now she looked—

He didn't care how she looked. She was under his

protection for the duration and he wouldn't forget that no matter how tantalizing Miss Miami Beach looked!

Jason knocked on the door and pushed it open, carrying two plates covered with aluminum foil.

"Food, Mike. Hi, Savannah. We're going to miss you at dinner tonight," he said easily.

"Hi, Jason. Let me help."

She sprang up from her chair and hurried to take the dishes from the man. "You know how lovers are, we want to spend some time alone together."

She cocked her head and gave Mike a sultry look as she followed Hank into the dining room. Placing the plates down on the large table, she turned back.

Lovers? Mike stood and clamped down hard on the urge to cover her mouth before she said something else outrageous. They were pretend lovers. She sure threw herself into the role quickly. Was it from practice?

Did she have someone waiting in Florida? It hadn't shown in her file. The marshal's service had compiled the file to see who might have a reason for wanting to do her harm. Only Ramirez's name popped up. No current boyfriend showed.

"Well, we don't blame Mike a bit. Only we don't think he should be so selfish," Jason said.

She laughed and patted his arm. "Tomorrow I'll come for dinner. And hope I can remember everyone's names."

Jason glanced at Mike's scowling face and then back to Savannah's sunny expression. "We'll be glad to have you." After a noticeable pause he nodded toward Mike. "You, too, Mike, if you bring a smile."

"Get out, Jason. Thanks for dinner."

The cowboy chuckled and left.

"Ready to eat?" she asked brightly, ignoring the growing storm clouds.

If Mike wanted to be a grouch to everyone, let him. She'd enjoy the meal, even if she missed the company of the other cowboys she'd enjoyed last night. Something told her Mike wouldn't be as entertaining.

He crossed the short entryway and moved into the dining room, crowding Savannah back against the table, his eyes mocking hers.

"Is eating all you want, lover? Sure you don't want to take advantage of our time alone?"

She pushed his chest, he didn't move. Solid muscle beneath his shirt, his warmth seeped into her fingertips. Slowly her eyes moved upward until she met his gaze.

"Aren't you the one who started this charade? Aren't you the one who said we shouldn't do anything to give rise to questions about the reality of the engagement? You said we'd eat here tonight, I wanted to go to the bunkhouse. Nothing personal, Marshal, but I'm tired of being alone with you all day. First you're quiet, then you're bossy. Nothing I do pleases you and I was hoping for some laughter and good conversation. At the very least, I'd hear about the cowboys' day and forget a bit that my entire life has been turned topsy-turvey."

His hands covered hers as they rested on his chest.

"Tomorrow we'll eat with the men. I realize how alone you must feel. Being here is for your protection, but a woman used to bright lights and lots of excitement must feel stifled here."

Stifled wasn't how she felt with his hands holding hers

against his hard chest. Burning hot was more like it. Mesmerized by his touch, by the look in his dark eyes, entranced with the thought of his lips covering hers again, definitely burning hot.

Desire grew as he held her. She took a breath and instantly realized her mistake. His scent enveloped her. So unlike the feminine perfumes and cologne she was used to, he smelled of leather and pine, of sun and heat and masculine strength.

Her heart began tripping faster in her chest and she wondered if he could feel her pulse increase.

"We'd better eat while it's hot." Was that whisper her voice?

Tugging her hands free, she slid sideways along the table when he released her. Without a backward glance, she scurried to the kitchen. They needed silverware and something to drink. Iced water sounded about right. Maybe she'd douse herself with it while she was at it.

Where was a freezing cold river when she needed it?

Grateful for the chance to be away from the powerful appeal of Marshal Mike Black, Savannah stalled as long as she could. Afraid he'd come looking for her, and make some mocking comment, she finally drew a deep breath and headed back to the dining room.

Mike stood at the head of the table, her plate to his right. He'd removed the foil from both their meals and Savannah could see the steam drifting up.

"Water all right?" she asked, setting down a full glass before each plate.

"Sure."

He waited while she placed the silverware and napkins,

then drew out her chair. She sat down hard, trying to think of something beside how his hands had felt holding hers, how her senses swam around him.

"Did you read this afternoon?" he asked as he sat.

"Yes. I finished the book. Do you have another by him?" she said, determined to keep the conversation strictly on the impersonal.

"Sure. I think Tom has all his books. I'll look after dinner."

Savannah had attended enough business dinners to have mastered the art of keeping the conversation along the lines she wanted—safe topics like what they enjoyed in books and movies, their favorite foods, and who they thought might be president at the next election. As soon as they finished, Savannah swept up the plates and headed for the kitchen. She washed, Mike dried, which took all of five minutes.

She could escape now. Hide in her room until morning.

"If you could get me a book, I'd like to read another one," she said as they walked out of the kitchen.

"No television?"

"Not tonight. I'm a bit stiff from the ride today. I think I'd rather lie down."

Alone, away from his disturbing presence.

"You'll probably be stiff for a few days. Until we go riding again. Would you like to go tomorrow?"

She didn't hesitate. "Yes. I liked it. I might as well get something from being on a ranch."

"I'll get you a book."

Ten minutes later Savannah had donned Mike's sweatshirt to sleep in and crawled into bed. Her legs ached and were tender near the knees where the wet jeans had rubbed.

She felt proud of her accomplishment, however. Prior to today she'd never even sat on a horse. If they rode every day, she'd be a pro by the end of the three weeks.

Maybe Mike had been right. Maybe she should try to treat this as a vacation—take advantage of everything she could see and do that'd be different from Miami.

In three weeks, she'd testify and then resume her life.

When the cry came that night, Mike halfway expected it. He'd gone to bed a few hours earlier, but had only taken off his shirt and lay on the top of the bed. It felt cool, but the house was comfortable enough. Mike left his door open and when he heard Savannah cry out, he reached her in seconds. A quick scan showed him the room was empty except for the woman tossing around in the bed.

He sat on the edge of the mattress. Shaking her gently, he called her name.

She came awake quickly. There was enough light spilling in from the hall for her to see him. The bewilderment faded as she realized where she was, who was there with her.

"Another nightmare?" he asked softly, rubbing her shoulders gently. His sweatshirt swallowed her, making her seem like a little girl in dress-ups.

She shuddered and wiped her eyes. "I guess."

Giving into temptation, he picked her up, blankets and all and sat on the chair near the window. It creaked ominously, but held. Wrapping his arms around her, he placed her head against his shoulder.

"Tell me about the nightmare. Talking it out helps sometimes."

"It always starts with the shooting. I saw Ramirez shoot the gun, you know. I saw all the blood explode from his victim. In my dream blood covers everything, the street, the cars, and it's trying to get me like a flood I can't out run. Then I'm running and he's running after me. I'm so scared in the dream. I can't run fast enough. The blood keeps coming closer and closer and he keeps coming and...and then you woke me up."

"Have you had this dream often?"

She nodded, her silky hair rubbing against his bare shoulder.

"What happens if no one wakes you up?"

"I usually hear the sound of a gun and then feel as if I'm dead. It's awful. I hate it. I hate everything about it. Did you know I just went to get some ice cream? I could have stayed home that night, but I had a craving for mint chocolate chip ice cream and just ran to the nearby store to get some."

"Luck of the draw, Savannah. Hang in there for a little longer. We'll get you through this and then you can go back to your normal life."

"If there's anything left."

"What do you mean?"

"I'm not sure the owner of the boutique will hold my job this long. It's been over six months of hiding and before that I missed days because of the threats and the attempts on my life. I was in negotiations with her to buy into the business. That could all be gone. I know my house plants are dead. My friends probably think I've left Miami for good. Once the district attorney realized I was in danger, he whisked me into hiding. No time to let anyone know or to make plans."

"You can buy new plants, explain to your boss and your friends. Things'll go back to the way they were before."

She sighed, feeling oddly content. For the first time that she could remember, someone held her, comforted her.

"This is nice. I'm sorry I woke you up," she said softly, loathed to leave the comfort of his arms, but knowing she needed to get back to bed and let him get some sleep.

"I wasn't asleep yet. Sometimes on a case I pull the night watch and stay up all night. You feeling better?"

She nodded, rubbing her hair against his skin again. "I should get up."

He smiled. She hadn't moved a muscle—only saying what she thought she should.

"In a little while. I'm not sleepy. So if you want to stay right here for a bit, that's fine."

Her hand covered his biceps, reveling in the feel of his hard muscle beneath the taut skin. "Aren't you cold?"

"With you and all these blankets? I don't think so."

She smiled, letting her hand stay on his arm. Wishing the night could go on forever, she imprinted every aspect on her memory.

"It must be wonderful to have someone there for you all the time like your brothers," she said softly. "I've been alone most of my life."

"Not when you were a kid," he said. "And you're not much more than that now."

She smiled, feeling safe and cherished in the dark room with the man sworn to guard her life.

"My mother died when I was a little girl. My dad couldn't afford child care. I spent a lot of my life locked safely in the house. He wasn't a very good provider. We didn't have much. And when he got a bit of money, he drank it away. He really missed Mama. More than he cared about me, I guess. Then Child Protective Services stepped in and it was a series of foster homes."

"So we have a bit in common, fiancée."

"Like what?" She smiled in the dark at his use of the word. What would it be like to be engaged to him, or anyone? To commit her life to another, have someone commit to her?

"My father wasn't much of a father, either. He married four times, had women on the side, and never spent much time with any of his sons. Had one son by each wife but the last one, then neglected both wife and son."

"I plan to do things differently if I ever get married and have kids. I planned to be the best mom in the world. But I don't think I'll get married. Robert cured that romantic notion," Savannah said softly. "Once you lose trust, it's hard to get it back."

"Tell me about Robert," Mike said softly.

"You don't really want to know. It's late, I should let you get to bed."

His arms tightened fractionally around her. "Tell me about Robert," he said more strongly.

"We met in college. I loved him and thought he loved me. But he didn't."

"How do you know that?"

"He said as much at the end. But I should have known from the beginning. He didn't like my clothes, my hairstyle, the way I talked sometimes. He was always trying to change me."

She was quiet for a moment, remembering.

"Like me," Mike said heavily.

She shrugged. "You don't like much about me, but at least you aren't trying to change me, just get through the days until I have to leave."

"I don't dislike you. I'm trying to do a job here. One way to keep someone safe is to make sure to keep a low profile so no one can find them. You're the most alive person I've met in a while. After all you've been through, you still act as naive as an innocent babe. There're bad men out there trying to kill you to stop you from testifying. The better hidden you are, the better I'll be at keeping you safe. And a low profile doesn't mean having every cowboy in twenty miles fall for you, talk about you, mention you in town. That could expose our location."

"I don't flirt with the cowboys. I'm truly fascinated in what they have to say. I want to learn more about ranch life. It's so different from the beach crowd I'm used to. But if I smile, you start yelling."

He groaned and hugged her tighter.

"Your smile is enough to light up the world. You're going to have every cowboy in that bunkhouse fall in love with you. Then they'll get to town and start talking and the next thing we know, we'll have cowboys from neighboring ranches coming to call."

She laughed softly. "You're trying to make me feel good, Marshal, thank you."

"Do you suppose that you might call me Mike?" he said.

She leaned back until she could see his face—all angles and planes in the dim light from the hall. She saw the gleam of his eyes, couldn't tell what he felt, or what he meant by asking her to call him Mike.

"Yes, I could, Mike," she said clearly.

His hand cradled her head, his fingers threading in her soft hair as he pulled her back to his shoulder.

Savannah held her breath, gradually relaxing. She'd never been held like this and the sensations coursing through her body did nothing to induce sleep. She relished this contact, enjoyed the shock of feelings that poured through her, driving the last vestiges of the dream away, filling her with the reaffirmation of life. She didn't know enough to entice him to kiss her again, couldn't think of anything as all conscious thought fled and only the shimmer of awareness filled her.

For a moment, doubt surfaced. Maybe she didn't have her life mapped out successfully. She liked being held. She liked sharing in the dark of the night. When this was all over, she was going to seriously consider getting involved with someone. Even if she never fell in love again, she liked feeling connected.

Six

Warmth woke Savannah the next morning. She slowly came awake. Sometime in the night she'd kicked off the covers and now she felt the sun blazing through her window on her bare legs. Sitting up, she stretched, surprised to see the sun so high in the sky. How late was it? Glancing at the small clock on the dresser, she couldn't believe it—after ten. How had Mike let her sleep so late?

Memories of last night flooded. She recalled every second from the moment he'd awakened her from the nightmare until he'd lifted her up and tucked her back into her bed. He'd been quite unlike the taciturn marshal she thought she knew.

For a while, he'd been caring. Almost loving.

Yeah, right, almost loving surely described that hardheaded man. She went to the window and opened it. The air outside felt marginally cooler than her room. The puffy clouds from yesterday were gone-the sky a deep blue. She drew in a breath of the fresh warm air and marveled at how hot the day already felt. If they'd had this warmth yesterday, their foray into the creek might not have been so bad.

Savannah debated wearing the shorts she'd purchased in Laramie. In the end, she opted for the jeans. It felt warm, but she wasn't sure she could trust the Wyoming weather. Just yesterday she'd been cold. The weather was certainly unpredictable. Not like at home.

If it grew warmer later, she'd change into her bathing suit and take advantage of the sun. But first, she needed to investigate the whereabouts of one U.S. Deputy Marshal who was supposed to be guarding her.

Trying to decide what her attitude should be when she found him, she ventured forth. Should she be breezy and ignore last night?

Or was he expecting sweet and grateful?

She grinned. Breezy was definitely the tack she'd take. She certainly didn't want him to guess how much it meant to her to have someone hold her for once, to offer comfort against the fears of the dark. She'd been on her own for a long time. Long before her father died, she'd been alone. During her adult life, she'd never once had anyone to console her when things got rough or rejoice with her when things went well.

Not even Robert.

Rubbing her chest in a familiar way, she stopped in the doorway to the living room. No Mike. And she suddenly realized she rubbed her chest for no reason. The familiar ache she usually experienced when thinking about Robert was missing.

She stood still. Was she finally over the man? Over the disappointment and aching hurt that once engulfed her?

Looking back, objectively at last, she saw that she'd been fooling herself. Trying to make herself into someone to love, she'd tried too hard to be someone she was not. Robert hadn't loved her. She should have seen it from the beginning.

And if she hadn't been so caught up in her romantic dreams, maybe she would have.

There was nothing romantic about Mike Black. And yet he definitely held attraction for her. She wanted to learn every little bit about him.

In this case she had no illusions. There was nothing between them but some hot attraction. They'd spend some time together until she returned to Miami. And it'd then be over.

The ache reappeared. This time stronger than before. Brushing it aside as nonsense, she searched the rest of the house. He was not to be found.

Opening the door, Savannah glanced around the yard. She saw no one. Feeling daring at venturing out at last on her own, she walked to the bunkhouse. Two cowboys sat at the table, papers spread out before them. The fragrance of hot coffee permeated the room.

"Good morning," she said.

"Hey, Savannah."

"Good morning, Savannah. Want coffee?"

"I want something to eat. Can I fix it myself?"

"Jason's still in there, making a stew for dinner. He'll fix something for you."

She smiled and walked back to the kitchen. She wasn't sure if that was Pete or Marc, so didn't call him by name. She thought she'd remembered their names by now, but was still unsure. Steve she recognized, he'd been the first to greet her.

"Hi, Jason. Sorry I'm so late. Can I get something to eat?" Savannah said, entering the kitchen.

"Sure thing, Savannah. Mike said you needed to sleep in today. I saved you some hot cakes. Have a seat."

A half hour later Savannah was mopping up the last drop of the syrup with her last pancake when Mike entered. She and Jason has been chatting as he worked and she ate. The other cowboys had long gone back to work and the cook hadn't minded her keeping him company in the kitchen.

"Sleep all right?" Mike asked, his eyes assessing her.

Feeling the color rise in her cheeks, Savannah nodded. So much for breezy. He just looked at her and she felt as shy as a schoolgirl. Last night seemed so intimate. He'd held her for comfort. She'd shared a bit of her past. Why did the darkness make that easier?

"Yes, thank you. I didn't mean to sleep so late."

"No problem. I'm working in the barn. Will you be all right on your own this morning? We can go riding after lunch."

"Sure. I don't need a baby-sitter," she said. "I'd like that book you said you'd get me."

"It's in the office. On the shelves between the windows. Pick out one you want." His eyes never left hers.

Jason cleared his throat. When Mike looked at him, he grinned. "Just wanted you two to remember I'm here."

Mike scowled and turned, leaving without another word. He was playing a part, that's all. It was a foolish charade. If he had a bit of sense, he'd tell the men why they were here, swear them all to secrecy and forget the stupid charade.

But then he'd have no reason to touch her, to stay near her. Even to kiss her again.

He reset his hat. He had no business kissing her for any reason. She was a woman. That in itself was enough to warn him. He'd seen the results of becoming involved with any woman. He hadn't forgotten Amy. Nor the results of his father's many marriages. Women were to be enjoyed and then left. He certainly didn't need the complications they brought.

Although Savannah seemed to be more alone than other woman he knew. Alone and vulnerable. Maybe his brother Conner was right, maybe he had a white knight complex. He couldn't save Savannah from anything but the men after her.

Once the trial ended, she'd go back to her life in Miami and he'd stay in Denver. They were worlds apart and not only geographically.

She radiated sex appeal. He tried to keep a low profile to better do his job. She liked people-apparently men in particular. She flirted and laughed and about drove him crazy with her sexy body and cloud of wild silky hair. Last night that hair had rubbed against his bare chest He'd wanted to thread his fingers through the tresses and savor the sensation all night long. He had held himself aloof until he thought he would explode with desire.

But he'd put her chastely in her bed and left when she fell asleep. He knew his duty and would do it, no matter how hard it proved.

The sooner she returned to Florida, the better. Then he'd forget the pretty blond beauty and resume his solitary life. The way he liked things.

He paused for a moment outside the barn, wondering if he'd ever forget her.

Savannah frowned at the bathing suit. She'd grabbed it as they flew through the store on their whirlwind shopping spree. It was a one piece suit in shiny blue with the legs cut high and the top cut low. Still, it covered more than her bikini. She debated the wisdom of sunbathing in it. If she stayed out too long, she'd have tan lines where she hadn't had them before.

Better than her tan fading away all together, she decided.

Getting a towel from the bathroom, she ventured forth to the office. If she could find another Louis L'Amour book, she'd read for a while. When she entered the office she was struck at how neat it appeared.

Obviously Tom Black liked a tidy space, neat and organized, knowing exactly where everything was. She admired that. Her own office was neat and tidy. She prided herself on her organization skills and liked that in others.

The books in the case between the window showed evidence of being much loved and well-read. She skimmed the titles on the spines, smiling at the limited selection. Most were Westerns, with a few nonfiction books on cattle and horses—not unexpected in a rancher's library.

She selected another L'Amour book, and went to find a sunny spot outside.

"What the heck do you think you're doing?" Mike's hard voice startled Savannah an hour or so later.

She rolled over and sat up, holding the front of her suit to her chest. She'd taken down the straps to avoid tan lines.

Blinking up into his furious face, she was surprised to see anger.

"I'm sunbathing-reading. Why?"

What was wrong, hadn't he said she could go out by herself as long as she stayed near the house or barn?

"Why? Look at you!" His eyes raked her. "You have on about three square inches of material. There are a dozen men with their tongues hanging out because you're lying here with practically nothing on. This isn't Miami Beach!"

He stood beside her, as if he could block the view from the corral. Her legs went on forever, her back sheened with perspiration, glowing like honey. She'd pulled her hair up in a topknot that already slipped, falling around her ears. And he swore the sun had bleached it even lighter.

Savannah scrambled to her feet, no easy feat holding the front of her suit plastered against her. She should have left the straps up. Standing at last, she glared at the man.

"I am wearing a perfectly respectable bathing suit, which happens to cover a lot more than my bikini at home. I'm lying in the front yard of the house, not in the middle of the corral. I'm minding my own business and—"

"And driving every man in sight crazy."

She paused. "Every man?" she drawled, wondering if she were driving Mike crazy.

He caught her meaning. His gaze held hers for a moment.

"Every man," he repeated deliberately, his eyes steady.

She smiled.

He scowled even more darkly. Stepping closer, he leaned over until his face blocked the sun.

"Is that your game, Ms. Adams, drive the men crazy? Or is this more personal?"

"More personal?" Was that throaty sound her voice?

"Are you on some kind of mission to tempt the marshal to fall prey to your charms?"

"Do you think I could do that?" Deliberately she licked her lips, her eyes holding his.

"I know you could do that! The question is, are you trying?"

She cocked her head to one side. "Now why would I do

such a thing?"

She wanted to bat her lashes, but settled for one slow blink, then met his gaze boldly, challengingly. Let him think what he would.

"Don't bait me, Savannah," he warned ominously.

She shook her head, her eyes sparkling. "I was just sunbathing. Besides, didn't we decide yesterday that neither of us is susceptible to the other?"

She lied, she was extremely susceptible. It took a tremendous amount of willpower to keep from reaching out to rub the frown line away from his eyes, to keep her hands to herself, rather than feeling that warmth and strength she'd discovered last night.

"You'd try a saint in that getup. And I'm not a saint, Savannah."

His finger traced her bare neck, from her hairline to her throat. Fire trailed where his finger touched.

"I'll have you know this suit covers a lot more than the essentials. You just like your women in jeans and long-sleeve shirts that button to the neck," she said recklessly, licking her lips in a blatant attempt at seduction.

His eyes darkened. "I don't have women. I told you, I'm immune."

"Right."

Slowly she slipped one arm into the strap of the suit. His eyes followed her movement as she eased the material up over her shoulder. Once done, she slipped the other arm into its strap. Her eyes watched as his traced each move. He stood between her and the sun, but she could feel the heat from his body, blazing hotter than that of the sun.

One of the cowboys whistled.

Mike turned and glared at the culprit. Snatching up Savannah's towel, he draped it over her shoulders and held it together. His fingers rested on the valley between her breasts. She didn't move a muscle, catching her breath at the exquisite tingle that spread throughout her.

"Blast it!" he said, yanking his hand away from her damp skin. "Go inside and put on some clothes."

"I'm not finished sunbathing. I want to keep my tan."

"And I want to keep my sanity. Go put on some clothes!"

Savannah glanced over toward the corral. Three cowboys leaned against the fence, wide grins on their faces as they watched the scene. She looked up at Mike and smiled boldly. Reaching up, she let her hand rest on his neck.

"You do the part of a jealous lover well, Marshal. I assume this is all for the benefit of those cowboys. But you don't own me. Even if this engagement were real, I'd be entitled to sunbathe when and where I want."

She tugged against him and he leaned closer until she reached up and brushed her lips against his.

"Keep in the role, darlin'," she said as her lips touched his.

She knew she played with fire, but didn't care. She'd never felt like this, daring and dangerous. Their charade offered the perfect excuse and she flung herself into the role.

In a flash his arms came around her and pulled her tight.

"Like this, *darling?*"

"You do play the role so well," she replied, snuggling close, feeling totally reckless.

Her entire world had been knocked askew, why not take the role assigned her and run with it? Both knew they were

111

immune to any lasting attraction or danger of falling in love. Why not enjoy the charade?

He gave her no time to think further. His kiss was hot, almost explosive. Savannah forgot about provoking him, forgot about their audience, forgot everything but the wild sensations that rushed through her as his lips covered hers, as his tongue teased its way into her mouth. She clung to him like a drowning swimmer to a life ring while the world swirled around her.

Mike drew a shaky breath when he pulled back a scant inch. "To continue the fantasy, we should move into the house now."

She blinked. For a moment she'd forgotten the game.

Was she in danger of forgetting her immunity? No, she didn't think so. Not with someone as bossy and demanding as he proved to be.

She reached down and scooped up her book, giving in before he made it a major confrontation. "Very well, Marshal, I concede this time. But if tomorrow is equally warm, I will come back out for the sun."

"I'll make sure every man on the ranch works away from the homestead tomorrow," he growled, following her closely as she headed for the house.

"Worried I'll bolt?" she asked, conscious of him hovering only inches behind her.

"No, enjoying the view of legs that go on forever."

She flushed with delight and embarrassment. Not used to compliments, she didn't know how to reply. She held her head high and marched into the house.

"I guess I'll go dress in those jeans you like so much."

He nodded, pausing inside the door. He'd thought the

snug jeans bad enough until he saw her in that skimpy bathing suit. And it covered more than her bikini? He'd like to see that.

Rubbing his hand over his face, he walked to the office and slammed the door behind him. At the rate he was going, she'd drive him up a wall before the week ended and they had two more after that. Why wasn't life easy and predictable?

He'd thought this would be an easy assignment to guard a scared witness from Florida. Instead, he was fighting to keep his own sanity. The witness seemed anything but scared. And each time they came together, she seemed different. More feminine, more alluring

He'd seen the men watching her when he left from the barn. The impact of his anger and surge of protection surprised him. She was just a witness, someone *temporarily* assigned to him. He struggled to keep that in perspective.

For the first time he wished the marshals in Florida had been up to the job. Savannah Adams was trouble with a capital T.

The door to the office flew open. Savannah put her fists on her hips and glared at him. "This better, Marshal?"

Mike looked from the frothy pile of curls on top of her head to the gently rounded breasts behind the shirt that tied above that sexy triangle of tanned skin, down the long length of her legs encased in the stretch jeans she'd bought. Her feet were bare.

"I thought you were going to call me Mike," he said easily, refusing to give in to her provocation, refusing to acknowledge the ache of desire that simmered barely below the surface any time he saw her.

"Mike," she said through gritted teeth.

He smiled at the sight of her anger. Time she felt some of the upset she caused.

"Looks fine, Savannah. Ready to ride?"

She blinked. "I guess so." The winds gone from her sails, she lowered her hands. "I need to get my boots on. Just be a second."

She hurried to her room, confused by the man. One minute he acted like she'd committed a crime, the next he offered a treat. She looked forward to riding again. Her legs were stiff and sore from yesterday, but not enough to stop her. Stomping into boots, grabbing her water stained Stetson, she crammed it over the hair she'd piled on top of her hair. It left her neck bare.

Two cowboys in the barn teased her when she and Mike entered, making sly reference to her sunbathing. Mike's temper rose and he snapped out orders for the horses. The men laughed good-naturedly and nudged each other.

"Guards his woman pretty well, wouldn't you say?" Steve asked, chuckling at the glare on Mike's face.

Savannah laughed. She looked at Mike. "A woman loves to be cherished. You guys should try it sometime."

"I'm not getting hooked up with a woman," Steve protested. "Too many around to narrow the field to just one."

"Until you find the right one," she sassed back.

"Maybe you're her and already taken," he teased as he pulled the cinch tight.

Mike came behind Savannah and placed his hands on her waist, lifting her to the saddle.

"Whoa, oh, you scared me," she said as she sat hard on

the seat. "I could have managed."

"No problem. See you boys later." He mounted his own horse and rode from the barn.

"Thanks, Steve. See you at dinner." Savannah urged her horse to follow Mike, stretching muscles a bit, trying to ease the stiffness.

"Where are we going today?" she asked when she caught up. "I didn't bring my suit, so I guess swimming's out. Not that you let that stop you yesterday."

She smiled again at the memory. In retrospect it had been amusing.

"You wanted to ride, let's ride." He kicked his horse and the animal took off like a shot, Savannah's gelding in close pursuit.

She bounced all over the saddle, grasping the mane with one hand, the saddle horn with the other, holding on to the reins through instinct. Her hat bobbed off and flew behind her. The sun blazed down almost blinding her, the wind in her face caused her eyes to water, her hair to escape the clip and whip around her face. She clung to the horse afraid every second would be her last one before tumbling to the ground—a long way down.

Finally she caught enough of the rhythm to release the mane and yank back on the reins. The horse stopped so suddenly she almost flew over his neck. Her fist surrounding the saddle horn cushioned the blow to her stomach. Shaking, she sat up and took a breath. Without further thought, she swung her leg over and dismounted.

"Sorry, Smoky, I'm not up to wild western riding. I think walking will suit me fine the rest of my visit."

She watched as Mike rode farther and farther away. In

only a moment he'd crest that hill and disappear over the far side. And she didn't care. She'd almost been *killed* and he'd kept riding.

Savannah turned and headed back toward the homestead, slipping the reins over the horse's head as she'd seen the cowboys do so she could lead the creature.

Walking proved awkward on the rough ground, but doggedly she persisted. After a few minutes, she spotted her hat. She made a beeline for it. She almost reached it when she heard the rhythmic beat of a horse. Glancing over her shoulder, she saw Mike riding right toward her. Shrugging, she continued toward her hat.

"Did you fall off? Are you all right?" he asked as he drew near. Pulling his horse into a short stop, he dismounted and tossed the reins negligently on the ground before hurrying to Savannah.

"I did not fall, no thanks to you. I don't know how to ride a horse at a full gallop. You're lucky I didn't fall. What would the prosecution do if their key witness turned up dead?"

She reached down and snatched up her hat. Slamming it against her thigh to dislodge the dust, she released some of her anger and fear. She wished she could hit him over the head with it instead.

He took a deep breath, lifted his hat and ran his fingers through his hair before replacing it. Mike turned and gazed off toward the horizon, the muscles in his cheek clenching.

"I shouldn't have started off like that. I'm sorry. I wouldn't have you get hurt for anything." He hesitated a moment. "I was angry."

"Yeah, well, what else is new? You've been angry since

you picked me up. If you didn't want the assignment, you should have told your boss."

He looked at her. "Is that what you think? That I didn't want the assignment?"

"What should I think?" She put her hat on, tucking up her hair, glad for the shade from the brim. The sun shone so bright. The air that stirred around them was hot and fragrant with the scent of grass.

She breathed deeply, knowing she'd forever remember this ranch, this man, this moment if she ever smelled dust or horses or drying grass again.

"You should think that my job is to protect you against the men who are after you. You should be doing everything you can to help me in that assignment, instead of flaunting yourself to all the men on the ranch."

"You arrogant jerk. I'm tired of this theme. Once and for all, I'm not flaunting myself to anyone. I'm being friendly. Don't you have any friendly people in your life, Marshal, that you can recognize friendliness when you see it?"

She turned and started off again. It couldn't be that far to the barn. They'd only been riding for a couple of minutes before Mike took off.

"Where are you going?"

"Back to the ranch."

She smiled. Now she sounded like an old-time western movie character. In her wildest dreams she never thought she'd actually say something like that.

"Come riding."

"No, thanks. I'll ask one of the men to teach me how to ride in the corral before I venture off into the wild blue yonder. A sedate walk like yesterday is one thing. I'm not up to racing across the prairie like a tornado."

Mike took several steps until he caught up with her. His hand on her arm stopped her and Savannah looked up at him. "Now what?"

"I'll show you how to ride. I forgot you didn't know how."

"Trevor gave me a few basic pointers when he saddled the horse yesterday, that's all I've had. I expect you started riding when you were three."

He smiled at that and nodded.

She caught her breath.

When he smiled, there was nothing on earth she wanted to do but lose herself in him. His eyes softened, his dimple peeked out. She could feel her heart melt. It wasn't fair. She wanted to stay angry, to keep her distance. One smile melted her resistance and she knew she'd give in to anything he asked if he'd smile a bit more often.

"I'll show you how to ride," he said softly. "I can teach you."

Warily she studied him. "Why?"

"To keep up our charade, why else?" he said, flicking a finger against her rosy cheeks. "Did you get too much sun today? It can be deceiving up here. We're at a higher elevation that Miami, not as much atmosphere to protect you."

She resisted the urge to lean her cheek against his hand. "I'll take care of sunbathing, you take care of teaching me to ride."

"Deal. But let's at least ride back to the corral. Walking's hard in boots."

"And cowboys would rather ride than anything, right?" she said.

"Not anything." He mumbled as he took her reins and flipped them back to the gelding's neck. "Come on, mount up."

She started to say she could manage on her own, but kept her mouth shut. She normally did everything for herself. If Mike wanted to lift her up, she'd let him. She liked his hands on her waist, liked feeling the surge of power in his muscles as he lifted her to the horse.

Who said a tough Miami businesswoman couldn't be a sucker for a strong cowboy type? Even if only as a charade.

"Back already?" Steve asked when they rode into the barnyard.

"Savannah wants to practice different gaits in the corral. Once she's comfortable then we'll go back out."

"Sure thing." Steve hurried over to the corral and opened the gate. Two horses inside looked up.

"Can I ride with them in there?" she asked nervously.

"Steve, take them out, would you?" Mike asked.

Steve grinned. "Sure thing."

In only five minutes Mike patiently began teaching Savannah what she needed to know to ride the different gaits. An hour later she began to feel confident enough to try without Mike beside her.

"Want to go out now?" he asked as she successfully circled the corral for the tenth time at the lope.

"No thanks. I want to get off this fool horse and go soak in a hot bath. My legs feel like cooked spaghetti."

He chuckled. "And you haven't even tried to stand on them."

She smiled in return, delighting in the expression on his face. Then her smile faded. For one stabbing moment she wished she could get a picture of him to take back with her.

So she could show the other women at work, show her friends.

So she'd never forget his smile.

She wondered if looking at his picture years down the road would bring the same quivering sensation to her heart, would give her this vague feeling of longing that threatened to swamp her. Could a mere picture cause the same sensations being around him did?

"Are you all right?" he asked.

She nodded and looked away. Riding to the fence, she dismounted and promptly sank to the ground. The dirt was soft, churned up and light enough to float about her in the cloud of dust she'd created.

Mike laughed. "Told you."

She smiled and leaned back on her hands, gazing up at him. "So you did. But right now I don't care. I can hardly move. I might just stay here until dark."

He dismounted and tied his horse and hers to the fence. "Not a chance, sweetheart. Come on, I'll give you a lift." He reached down and scooped her up. Settling her against his chest, he headed for the gate.

"What are you doing? Put me down. I can walk. I just need to get some feeling in my legs."

"Put your arm around my neck and hold on. I'll take you to the house."

"More macho role playing?" she asked, encircling his neck with her arm, her other hand resting against his chest. The strength of his muscles was evident beneath his shirt and she flexed her fingers.

"Open the gate." He dipped a bit until she reached the latch. Once through, he turned so she could close it.

Savannah giggled softly. "This is silly, Mike. I can walk."

"Problems?" Steve called from the barn door.

"Nothing I can't handle," Mike replied, heading straight for the house, hoping it was the truth.

Seven

Two weeks later Savannah once again sank blissfully into a warm bath and sighed in pleasure. The contrast to the hot dusty ride she and Mike just finished was sublime. Slowly she let her body relax, soothed by the caressing touch of the water. The warmth eased her aching muscles.

Gingerly she stretched out one leg, winced and bent her knee. Riding used muscles she didn't even know she had. But she was getting used to it. Since that day when he'd taught her the different gaits, how to sit the saddle, hold the reins, she'd been practicing. Sometimes alone in the corral, sometimes on the range beside Mike. Maybe she wouldn't be an expert by the time she left, but she could ride.

Sliding down until her shoulders were covered with the warm water, she rested her head on the back edge of the tub. What day was it? How many more until she returned to Miami to testify at the trial? She counted. Still almost a week remained. Time raced or crawled, but never seemed to move at an even pace.

Usually it raced when she spent it in Mike's company. For a moment, she wished they'd met under different circum-stances. Would they have become friends?

She doubted it. Two weeks of constantly being around

him and she didn't know much more about him than when she started. Well, maybe a tad more. She knew where he went to college, that he liked to ski in winter and he could ride like he was part of the horse.

Still–if he'd come to Miami on vacation maybe things would be different. Without the responsibilities of his job, did he lighten up and give in to human traits, like wanting friendship or something more?

Or was he always so dedicated, intense? So determined not to repeat whatever had happened with that Amy woman he wasn't willing to bend an inch?

She tried to imagine him as a carefree tourist, enjoying the nightlife of Miami and the long stretches of sandy beaches. She couldn't bring a picture into focus. His dedication to his job overruled other traits.

When around the cowboys at dinner he seemed to relax, but not totally. He had a presence that constantly stood at alert. Ready for any danger, no matter how unexpected, he seemed to be more aware of his surroundings than anyone she'd ever met.

The water grew cool and Savannah stepped out, wincing again as her muscles protested. Riding wasn't pure fun as she'd once thought it'd be. Sore muscles suggested that she was better suited to Miami's beaches than Wyoming's trails.

Dressed again, she wandered around the house.

She was alone.

Frowning, she headed outside.

For a man who was supposed to guard her, he stayed away more and more. Ever since that night he'd held her after her nightmare.

She wasn't exactly counting the time since then, but it'd been twelve days. Would he ever loosen that ironclad control and relax around her?

She'd tried teasing, flirting, even an attempted seduction, but he merely clenched his jaw and walked away.

Where was he now? She knew she was safe on the ranch, Mike would never leave her unprotected if he thought she were in danger. But—

But what? Did she want him dogging her every step?

She rather thought she did.

He fascinated her. What made him tick? What made him want to put his life on the line to save others? Did he ever yearn to do anything else or was he content to be a Deputy U.S. Marshal for the rest of his life?

She knew it was a dangerous life. This assignment had turned out to be pretty innocuous, but his life would be in danger if the men after her found them.

She shivered at the thought. The marshal in Miami had training. He'd been brought down by the bomb.

Mike was proficient with the ranch work. Maybe one day he'd want to retire from law enforcement and return to work the place with his brother.

Would she ever know? When the assignment ended, so would her tie with Mike Black.

The afternoon breeze swirled and blew, stronger than previous days. She brushed the hair from her eyes and wished she'd pulled it back. Her hat kept part of it from blowing every which way, but she needed her hands to give some control.

Mike and Steve were in the corral. Hadn't they had enough riding for a day? She walked over, wondering what they were doing. As she approached, she saw Mike trying to mount a horse that didn't want to be ridden.

The horse sidestepped as he tried to swing into the saddle. Steve held the bridle near the bit, laughing, egging Mike on.

Savannah stood on the lower rail and rested her arms on the fence top, watching, curious to what would happen. In one fast blur, Mike flung himself into the saddle at the same time Steve let go and dashed away. The horse shivered for a moment, then lowered his head and lashed out with his back feet. Bucking and twisting, he became a blur of movement as he furiously tried to shake the man from his back.

Steve laughed and called out suggestions. He spotted Savannah and joined her, climbing up to sit on the top rail.

"Mike's good, but that horse is a wild one and Mike's been away from ranching for a while. Watch. Hey, Mike, settle him down!"

Savannah held her breath. Several times it looked as if Mike would leave the saddle, but each time he slammed down hard in the seat.

She could see the raw determination in his expression. It was an expression she'd grown more and more familiar with.

Fascinated with another aspect of her lawman, she watched, fear temporarily overridden by the excitement of the attempt of man to conquer a recalcitrant horse.

Two more cowboys joined them at the fence. Whistling and yelling comments, the commotion served to excite the horse even more. He whirled around kicking and shaking. He ran toward the fence as if to scrape off the rider. He kicked his back legs, his head tucked almost between his front hooves. Rising straight up, he twisted as his hoofs slammed into the ground. Nothing dislodged Mike, however.

The horse shone with sweat when he finally stopped. His head hung as he blew hard, his sides heaving. Mike patted his neck and gathered the reins. Slowly they moved forward at a walk.

The cowboys cheered.

Savannah began to breathe again. She became aware that she gripped the top rail tightly and consciously relaxed her fingers.

Fear for Mike's safety was replaced with a warmth of pride in his skill and accomplishment. He could have been seriously injured if thrown, but he'd stayed on. Maybe working at a ranch wasn't any safer than being a marshal. Not if the fool man took chances like this one.

"So how'd you like that, Eastern city slicker?" Steve asked, tugging on the brim of her Stetson.

She grinned up at him. "Great. A little scary, but exciting. You do that kind of thing, too?"

He laughed and shook his head. "Not anymore. But you'd be hard-pressed to find many cowboys who haven't done a rodeo event or two. Mostly when we're too young to know any better."

"He's lucky the fool horse didn't roll with him. He tried that with Jack a couple of weeks ago," Hank said, leaning against the fence.

Savannah shivered, still aware of how exciting it'd been, partly because the danger to the rider was real.

"So why do y'all do it?" she asked, turning to face the cowboys.

She wanted to rush to Mike's side and tell him how glad she was he was all right. How splendid he'd looked—perfectly at home on a wild horse's back.

She could imagine the scene that'd produce–his scathing words. She'd be more comfortable dealing with the others.

"No guts, no glory—you have to take chances to achieve a dream," Steve said, watching Mike.

"It's exciting," Trevor said, moving to stand beside Hank and Steve.

"You get so pumped up you think you can do anything," Hank added.

"Yeah, if you can make eight seconds."

"Eight seconds?" Savannah asked, trying to follow the conversation.

"That's the official time for rodeo bronc riding," Steve explained.

"But Mike stayed on longer than eight seconds. I know it was longer."

It had seemed endless especially each time one of the men commented on the possibility of his falling.

"Sure thing. This is the only way to get some horses broke to rein. But we're trying to make the horse get used to a human. In the rodeo events, we ride differently."

"Both are dangerous."

"But if you achieve your aim, it's worth it, whether it's a winning score, or a working horse, right?"

Mike urged the horse over to the rails. He might have expected Savannah to be right in the middle of the men. She listened to something Steve said with full attention, her big blue eyes fixed on him as if he were the most important thing in her world. Steve lapped it up, too. Mike didn't blame him.

He'd been the recipient of that hot gaze more times than

he cared to remember over the last couple of weeks. And every time, he'd felt an attraction and awareness stronger than the last.

Out of habit, he scanned the surroundings. Nothing out of the ordinary. He hadn't expected anything to be, but he constantly checked.

"Anyone want to ride this lamb?" he drawled, his eyes on Savannah.

She spun around and met his gaze, her wide sunny smile hitting him hard.

"I don't," she said quickly, laughing a bit. "But you were wonderful, Marshal. I never expected such hidden talent."

"Marshal?" Hank said with amusement. "My, aren't we formal?"

"She likes to keep reminding me, I think," Mike said quickly, trying to cover her slip. "Sometimes I wonder if the badge was the first attraction."

"Now, darling, how could you ever suspect that?" she replied, color staining her cheeks.

Mike knew she realized she'd forgotten their charade for a moment. But she came back fast. He felt almost proud of her for doing so.

"I'll take a turn," Trevor said. "Think he's too tired to put up a fuss?"

He climbed the fence and hopped down into the corral just as Mike dismounted.

"He's too tired today, but watch out tomorrow, he'll be back in fighting form."

Trevor swung easily up into the saddle and reined the horse away. Soon they were walking around the corral.

"He looks as docile as the horse I rode earlier,"

Savannah said, her thoughts in a tumble when Mike leaned against the fence to watch Trevor, his body so close to hers she could feel his heat.

"Once he learns who's boss, he'll be a good cow pony. He's got stamina and heart."

"Just needs to follow orders," she said softly so only he could hear.

Mike smiled. "That's right." He cut a glance in her direction. "Like some others I can think of."

She grinned back and tossed her head. "I'm not a horse, *darling*."

"That's for sure."

She wrinkled her nose and started to say something when Steve touched her shoulder.

"Want to come to the bunkhouse now and see those things from the rodeos I told you about?"

"Sure thing," she said, mimicking his constant reply.

He grinned and glanced at Mike. "Okay with you, Mike?"

"Fine with me. I need to get cleaned up anyway."

He looked back at the horse Trevor now rode as if he didn't care a bit what Savannah did. But he was aware of her. He could keep her in sight from the corner of his eye. When he turned to climb the fence, Savannah had tucked her hand into Steve's arm and the two of them were talking as they walked toward the bunkhouse. Hank fell into step on Savannah's other side.

Mike watched for a minute, then climbed out of the corral and headed for the house, a slow simmer of emotion building. He'd told her a hundred times not to flirt with the cowboys, but she flirted as naturally as most women breathed.

He didn't want anyone to question their mock engagement, he told himself. That's why he didn't want her flirting with other men. It had nothing to do with anything else! He wasn't jealous! That was a stupid emotion that occurred when a man cared about a woman. Savannah was only an assignment.

But the churning in his gut felt like jealousy. Of the ranch hands, of anyone on the receiving end of one of her smiles.

He'd call and check in again. See if anything new had arisen. If so, he wanted to know. But things had been safe so far. He thought their ruse of switching people at the airport and then having Sally go to Miami had probably been unnecessary. He wanted to make sure he knew if that ever changed.

When Mike entered the bunkhouse an hour later, Savannah was setting the dinner table. She looked up and nodded. Resuming the careful placement of the forks and knives, she said nothing.

"You all right?" she asked, pausing near the door to the kitchen.

"Why wouldn't I be?" His eyes narrowed as he studied her.

"That riding looked awfully dangerous this afternoon."

He shrugged. "It's kind of fun."

"You could have been hurt." Another place setting went down.

"Wasn't."

She looked up, exasperation written on her face. "I know that, but you could have been. Then who'd look after me?"

she said quickly. Let him think she worried about herself, about her own safety. It was safer than him questioning her concern for his safety.

"Ah, that's it, huh? Don't worry, Ms. Adams, the service would have provided someone for you within the day. And you are safe here. You have a dozen men all ready to slay dragons for you."

She pressed her lips tightly together to keep the words in. She hadn't meant to say what she did, hadn't meant to imply she was only concerned for herself.

But she dare not tell him how worried she was about his safety. Then he'd begin to wonder why and maybe even ask questions she didn't want to answer.

Putting the final fork in place, she studied the table. Was everything there? She couldn't think with him standing only a few feet away staring at her.

"What?" she said, lifting her eyes to meet his heated gaze.

"Did you have fun with Steve"

Her gaze met his, suspicion rampant. "He showed me some of his rodeo souvenirs."

"Like what?"

"He told me a bit about rodeos while you were riding that wild horse. He showed me a belt buckle he won and some pictures of him in different events. It was interesting."

"I bet he was flattered to have you drink in every word."

She flared in anger at his insinuation. "Jealous?" she snapped.

He crossed the room in three strides. No, he wasn't *jealous!* Capturing her cheeks gently in his palms, he threaded his fingers into the softness of her hair as he tilted her face up to his. Anger blazed in his gaze, but his hands stayed gentle against her skin.

"Not jealous, Savannah. There'd have to be something between us for me to feel jealous, right? I'm only concerned with keeping you safe. We have a cover story that you're in danger of blowing sky-high by your flirting with every one you come across."

Incensed at his insult, she opened her mouth to reply when she heard the footsteps in the other room, the jingle of spurs. Men began drifting in for dinner. She closed her mouth.

She'd speak to him later, when they were out of hearing of the others.

But she couldn't shake herself away from Mike. She grasped his wrists, her eyes locked with his. Her heart pounded in her chest, blood rushed through her veins, heating her to a fever pitch. His words didn't penetrate, not with the intensity he wanted.

She began to savor the feelings that shimmered through her. The tingling where his hands cradled her face, the shivers of electricity that seemed to race through her body. The stunning anticipation that bubbled up.

His hard eyes holding hers, he deliberately lowered his face until his lips touched hers.

But his kiss was cold. He made a statement, showing off for the men starting to infiltrate into the room—merely shoring up the pretense of an engagement. The spark between them was lacking. His kiss chilled her to the bone.

Raising his head, his look contemptuous, he released her and turned away.

Crushed, Savannah took a deep breath and plastered a bright smile on her face as the men began to speak to her. Could they tell how false it was? Did her rapidly beating heart show, did the disappointment and anger? She hoped not.

"Howdy, Savannah."

"Heard you went riding earlier today."

"Are you going to try that killer horse Mike rode?"

She shook her head and hurried into the kitchen, too shattered to say a word.

Mike made it perfectly clear that he had no use for her. He was only guarding her until time for her to testify. That parody of a kiss had been pure meanness. If he'd slapped her, he couldn't have upset her more.

She was growing to care for him. Prior to that kiss she might have suspected he was growing to care for her. Or at least liked her.

Now she didn't believe it. A simple "let's keep up the pretense" would have sufficed. She hadn't needed his mocking kiss. And that's what it had been. He had to know how much she reacted to his previous attention. He'd made his point loud and clear. He was not interested in her.

Savannah kept silent during dinner, so homesick she could cry. Once she returned to Miami, she'd never go out after dark. She wouldn't give in to cravings and run the risk of seeing anything that could disrupt the stable life she'd built herself.

Granted, she felt lonely sometimes, but better lonely than to put up with a man who mocked her feelings.

Savannah refused to look at Mike during the meal. It didn't go unnoticed by the men, but no one said a word. Steve took up stories about rodeos and soon the others joined in, each trying to outshine the other. While grateful for their attempts to interest her, she still craved the sanctuary of her room.

Other evenings she enjoyed the camaraderie of the cowboys. Now it only served to show how bereft her life was of close friends and relatives.

She had a small circle of friends, yet all but one of the women were married and their families came first. These men worked together, lived together and shared all their good times and bad. They looked out for each other. Even their teasing had a warm, caring feeling. She had never been part of a group that shared so much.

Refusing dessert, Savannah rose when Hank and Jason began to clear the dishes.

"I think I'll head back now. I'm still stiff from all the riding I did today."

She smiled politely and headed for the door.

"I'll walk you back." Mike rose and followed.

"That's not necessary," she replied frostily as he opened the door for her. "I'm sure I can make it all the way to the house alone."

He didn't reply, simply fell in step with her.

Neither spoke as they walked quickly to the ranch house. Mike stopped her at the door with a hand on her shoulder. He entered first and switched on lights. Quickly moving through the house while she waited just inside the door, he verified it was empty.

When he told her, she nodded, passed without speaking and went to her room. Closing the door quietly behind her, the tears that welled spilled down her cheeks. Flinging herself on the bed, she muffled her crying with her pillow.

She was so homesick! Desperately trying to keep quiet, she cried until the tears wouldn't come anymore. She cried for the lost time at work and maybe the lost opportunity to become a partner. She cried for the emptiness in her life—the fact no one waited somewhere wondering where she was, frantically worried about her.

And she cried for the man who only saw her as an assignment.

When the tears finally ended, she lay on the bed and tried to discover just where her life had become so muddled.

The shooting had changed everything, of course. Meeting Mike should have meant no more than meeting those marshals in Florida. But it did.

There was something about the man that called to her like no one had since Robert. And like Robert, Mike wasn't interested in her. He wanted her to change, stop her being who she was. And that she couldn't do.

Was it her lot in life to fall in love with men who didn't want her?

Fall in love? Was she falling in love with the taciturn, bossy, rude man who had total control over her life for the next few days, then would pack her off like an unwanted parcel?

No!

It did no good to lie to herself.

She was falling for Mike Black and there didn't seem to be anything she could do about it.

Listing his faults didn't help—quickly on the thought came the good aspects of the man. And overlying it all was the magnetic pull of physical attraction she'd never felt before. He overwhelmed her. Even with his cutting remarks, the pull remained. And when he charmed, there was no one like him.

Despite her red eyes, her unhappy thoughts, she smiled when she remembered falling in the river and the riding lessons, remembered how upset he'd been when he'd found her sunbathing, and the kiss that he'd given her then. She enjoyed riding, learning about cattle, joking with the men. Drawing the old bedspread over her, she drifted to sleep, thinking she was almost beginning to like Wyoming.

Savannah's normal sunny attitude returned by breakfast. She dressed quickly upon awakening and hurried to the bunkhouse. She didn't wait for Mike, not caring if he got mad that she went alone. They'd seen no sign of trouble in over two weeks and she felt as safe as she had before witnessing the murder.

"Morning, Savannah. You look chipper today," Jason said when she joined him in the huge kitchen. She'd greeted the men gathered around the dining table sipping coffee. A couple looked half asleep.

"I am. I'm going to sit in the sun today and do nothing. Every muscle in my legs aches," she complained with a bright smile.

"Nah, you need to get back on the horse, keep exercising those muscles to build them up."

Without thinking she replied, "Not me. I've been riding almost every day for weeks. I've had enough. I won't be riding after next week, so I'll give my legs a break and let them soak up some sun."

And probably make Mike angry at the same time. She almost relished his reaction. She didn't think he'd ignore her sunbathing.

Jason stared at her. "Why not?" he asked.

"Why not what?"

She poured herself a cup of coffee from the pot simmering on the stove. Cowboy coffee was strong enough to chew. But she was beginning to get use to it.

"Why won't you be riding after next week?"

"I'll be going home to Miami."

"But you'll be back," he said quietly.

She flushed, remembering too late the charade. Taking a sip of coffee, she tried desperately to come up with an answer that wouldn't be an out-and-out lie.

She liked Jason. She liked all the men who worked on the Bar B. But if she told them the truth, Mike would skin her alive.

"Thought that was part of the reason Mike brought you here, so you could see what was so important to him. He's a marshal during the year, but always comes home for vacations and holidays. I always thought that one day he'll give up law enforcement and settle down to raise a parcel of kids and help Tom with the ranch."

Savannah looked up, her eyes troubled.

"Maybe he will, but it won't be with me. I'm a beach person. I miss the ocean, the people, the diversity of Miami. I don't belong here, Jason. I know that and I think Mike knows that."

"You two had a fight, that was obvious at dinner. Don't throw away your whole future because of a fight, Savannah. Work things out with Mike."

She smiled and nodded, their deception weighing heavily on her.

These were nice people. They shouldn't be lied to.

Steve and Trevor came into the kitchen.

"Where's the grub?" Trevor grumbled, heading for the coffeepot.

"Whooee, we're cheerful first thing, aren't we?" Savannah said, grateful for the interruption. Jason had pressed too close to the truth.

"I need three cups of coffee before I'm halfway decent," Trevor said, swallowing gulps of the hot brew.

"And that's all he ever gets–halfway decent," Steve said, joking. He peered over Jason's shoulder. "I'm starved."

"Get yourself out of my kitchen. The food will be on the table in a few minutes. And you're always starving, Steve."

"Come keep me company, Savannah, so I can forget the weakness flooding me from lack of food."

She laughed and crossed the room with him. They sat at the long table in the dining room, others already seated, talking quietly, or staring at nothing as they drank their coffee.

"You and Mike haven't been off the ranch since you arrived. Come into town with us tonight. There's a great country band at the O.K. Corral. Do much Western dancing?"

She shook her head. "The kind of nightclubs I go to in Miami tend to play Latin music. We have a lot of Cubans in Miami, you know."

"Well, you'll never hear good music any younger."

"Good music—meaning country music?" She raised her eyebrows.

He chuckled. "The best there is. Come tonight and see."

"I don't think Mike would want to," she temporized

"What wouldn't Mike want to do?" the man asked,

standing in the doorway, the familiar disapproval evident in his expression.

She grinned at him, determined that the others would not suspect how much she longed to punch him—or kiss him.

"Steve suggested we go into town tonight to see some country band that's playing. I didn't think you'd want to."

"You're right." Mike pulled out a chair and sat down.

"Maybe you two are getting cabin fever," Steve said slowly, his eyes meeting, holding Mike's.

"Meaning?"

"I detect a slight chill in the air. Maybe you and Savannah need to get away for a bit, go into town, have dinner, stop by O.K. and dance a bit. We know you think the Bar B is the greatest, but maybe your beach bunny doesn't."

Mike met his gaze for another moment, then swung it to Savannah. "Complaining?"

"Not me."

For a moment she thought about going into town. About acting like a normal person for a few hours. Maybe shop a bit, see the different stores in town.

To eat dinner alone with Mike rather than surrounded by fourteen other men would be a treat. But only if he stopped scowling. And only if he thought it safe. No one knew where she was, no one would be looking for her in Laramie.

"There's enough to do here," he said.

"Sure is," she agreed, smiling brightly. "Immediately after breakfast, I plan to change into my bathing suit and lie in the sun."

She stared him straight in the eyes, deliberately daring him to challenge her.

Mike's "The heck you will," was drowned out by Trevor's louder voice. "I think that's a fine idea, Savannah. You could even go down by the river. It's not so hot now but later if it get hot, you could take a dip."

"Oh, no, you don't. I've already been in that barely melted ice you call a river."

The men laughed.

Mike kept silent, studying the defiance Savannah flaunted.

"Let me make a phone call this morning. Maybe Steve's right. We need a little time away from here," Mike said slowly.

The strain was telling, on both of them. If it was safe, it'd be good to get away for a bit, see a change of scenery.

Savannah looked up in surprise. For once she kept her mouth shut, afraid to say the least little thing that might cause Mike to reconsider. She smiled at him, a true, warm, happy smile. The thought of a few hours away from the ranch, away from the constant awareness of her prisoner-like status would be wonderful.

Happiness bubbled up and she threw herself into the conversation around the table.

Mike hung up the phone and stared out the window. Every indication pointed to the fact no one suspecting Savannah was not still hiding somewhere in Florida. His boss endorsed his idea of a trip into town to give the witness a break. There was nothing to hold them back, except his own reluctance to spend the day with her.

Here he had chores he could do. Others could entertain

her, much as it rubbed him the wrong way when she laughed and flirted with the men.

But a day alone with just Savannah might be more than he could take.

He couldn't forget how her face had lit up when he'd said he'd see about taking her out. A child at Christmas couldn't be more excited. He couldn't bear to see that happiness dashed if he told her no.

Sighing heavily, he rose and went to find her. She'd have her day in town. Anticipation and foreboding mingled as he walked toward the living room.

He found her pacing before the fireplace.

"Well, can we go?" she asked as soon as she spotted him.

"Yeah. Headquarters doesn't believe anyone has any idea you're not in Florida, much less in Wyoming. I think it'll be perfectly safe. But you have to follow orders, Savannah. If I suspect anything's going down, I'll take care of you, but you have to respond instantly to anything I tell you."

"Bossy," she murmured, snatching up her hat. Her smiling face met his as she nodded vigorously. "I'll be militarily perfect." She threw a snappy salute. "Thanks, Mike, I truly appreciate this!"

"Yeah."

Foreboding claimed him. The feelings that swamped him when around her meant nothing. When she was gone, they'd fade. He hoped he wasn't making a mistake.

He'd made one over a woman years ago and he didn't want history repeating itself.

Eight

They left the ranch an hour later. Mike had been vague about meeting the men that night at the local cowboy bar. For a start, he'd make sure Savannah spent the day however she wanted. He just hoped he'd last. Time enough later to decide on the evening.

The old Jeep wound its way down the mountain road and reached the straight section that led directly to Laramie. Savannah gazed out the window, avidly studying the scenery. She knew she wouldn't be this way again once she returned home. For a moment she almost regretted the thought.

Was she beginning to like Wyoming?

In the distance she spotted the beginning of the buildings of Laramie. The lofty cottonwoods that marked the older part of town provided the only stand of trees for miles. Rolling grass plains surrounded the town then spread out to the foot of the mountains.

There were no palm trees, no hint of salt in the air, only the dry heat and scent of grass. Yet there was an austere beauty to the setting. The mountains were unlike anything in Florida. And the openness was almost startling to one used to trees and shrubs and flowers everywhere.

"Have you ever been to Miami?" she asked as they

approached the town.

"No."

Mike hadn't said anything all the way in. She wondered what he was thinking about. Did he worry about keeping her safe? No, if he'd had any concerns, he never would have left the Bar B.

"Will you get a chance to go sightseeing when you take me home?"

"Doubt it."

"I could show you a bit," she offered diffidently.

He flicked her a glance. "We'll be arriving the night before the trial begins. They're selecting the jury this week. Once that's done, we'll get word and head for Miami. You'll be one of the first witnesses, but we'll keep you under tight security until we are sure you'll be safe. My job is to deliver you to Miami. Once that's over, I'll be returning home."

She swallowed. It sounded so cut-and-dried. Didn't it bother him at all that they wouldn't see each other after that?

"Take a vacation day and come to the beach with me."

He hesitated so long she thought he wouldn't reply.

"Why?" he asked at last.

"You've shown me parts of Wyoming. I never would have had the chance to see a ranch like I'm doing now. I want to return the favor."

That sounded reasonable. No matter how good a detective he might be, that wouldn't give anything away.

"This is business, Savannah. When you've testified, the threat to your life will be gone. Then the business between us will be finished."

"I see."

She stared blindly out the windshield. Of course for him

143

it was business. She was the only one foolish enough to feel something that didn't exist. She had a track record, after all, of falling for men who didn't really want her.

"Savannah—"

She turned to him and flashed a brilliant smile. Only she knew what it cost her.

"Don't worry about it, Marshal. Us Southerners are noted for our hospitality, I only wanted to show off my city after you'd shown me your ranch. I understand about business and all. Now, what are we going to see today? What boutiques are there in Laramie?"

"The university is the main attraction in Laramie. I don't know much about the stores."

"You went to the university here, didn't you?"

She remembered that from a conversation around the dinner table one night A tidbit of information to remember down the years.

"And studied law enforcement?"

"Criminology."

"Did your brothers go here, as well?"

"Yes."

She waited, but he said nothing further. Obviously if she wanted to get anything more, she'd have to ask. She wasn't sure she was up to it.

Mike drove through town and Savannah became intrigued. Laramie was quite different from Miami. For one thing, there were no tall buildings. The stores and office buildings were made of brick or stone, one or two stories high. The tallest building she spotted couldn't have been more than four or five floors. When he pulled to a stop beneath the widespread canopy of a cottonwood, she looked

144

at him inquiringly.

"We can walk from here. To see the university."

"Great."

If anyone had told her six months ago that one morning she'd be anxious to tour the University of Wyoming, she'd have thought them nuts. Now she wanted to learn more about Mike and this offered one opportunity–if she could get him talking.

By the time Savannah had been given his tour of the university, she knew a little more about Mike Black. While pointing out buildings he'd thrown in a few anecdotes about his days as a student. She wished she'd known him then. Had he been more carefree? She suspected his seriousness was innate and he used it to full advantage in the career he'd chosen.

"Now what?" she asked brightly as they headed toward the Jeep.

"Lunch, then we'll do whatever you want, within reason."

Savannah smiled. "Then I vote for shopping and a movie."

"Shopping?"

"Sure. Take that horrified look off your face, I want to check out what merchandise stores in town carry, how they display things. You never know when I'll get ideas I can use at my own place."

For a moment she wondered if she'd even have a job when she returned home, much less a shot at buying into the boutique. There was nothing to be done about it this afternoon. For the remainder of the day she was determined to enjoy herself and Mike's company.

Boldly tucking her hand into the crook of his elbow, she smiled up at him, leaning slightly against that hard body that so excited her. For a moment, she let the sensations sweep through her. She hoped she wouldn't forget what she wanted to say. Her hand tingled, waves of electricity coursed through her and her heartbeat increased.

"We won't buy anything, Marshal, I primarily want to look. Then when I've seen enough we'll go to the show. What movie would you like to see? I haven't seen anything in ages, obviously since it wasn't safe to be out and about. But we should be safe here, don't you think?"

"Of course or I wouldn't have brought you into town."

It hadn't been for her company, of that she was certain. He'd kept his distance all morning.

He unhooked her hand and reached for the door to the Jeep. Once Savannah settled, he slammed the door, rocking the vehicle. She blinked, wondering what had made him mad this time.

"Any place you want to eat?" he asked as he slid behind the wheel.

"Some place with greasy hamburgers and crisp fries. And a milkshake, a tall chocolate one. Onion rings, too, if they have them."

"Clog your arteries totally, why don't you?"

She grinned and leaned closer, confiding, "I'm starving for some good junk food. I eat a lot in the normal course of my life. I miss it. I think I'm suffering from withdrawal."

Mike stifled a groan and started the Jeep. The scent of honeysuckle filled the Jeep. If she leaned any closer, he'd forget keeping his distance and drag her all the way up against him. He wanted to kiss that sultry grin from her face and wipe the teasing lights from her eyes. One kiss would bring back that sexy, heavy-lidded look he'd seen a few times.

And one kiss would blow his resolution sky-high. He'd stay away from her as he wished he had stayed away from Amy. Once burned, anyone would think he'd have enough sense to avoid a second event. But his hormones threatened to overrule his head in this. He wanted to be around Savannah. He liked her sassy flirtation and he wanted more. He liked her almost childlike enthusiasm for ranching and horses. He liked seeing that half-wonder, half-delight expression when she came across something new.

Mike found a popular hamburger joint and waited for a couple of moments until a parking space became available.

"Want to eat inside or out here?" he asked as he turned off the engine.

Savannah looked into the small place, crowded with college students and one or two businessmen.

"Out here. Too crowded inside."

"I'll get the food and be right back. Don't go anywhere."

"Where would I go? I'm starving and you think I'm going someplace else? This looks like hamburger heaven. Do I—"

His finger covered her lips. "Shut up. I'll be right back."

Savannah watched him wade into the sea of humanity as her tongue brushed back and forth across her lips. He could have found a more effective way of getting her to shut up, she thought dreamily. He could have kissed her again.

Oh, that would have been great. She'd do much better to keep her distance and fight the attraction she felt. In no time she'd be back home and Wyoming would be nothing but a memory.

And if she wanted to escape with her heart intact, she had better remember that!

Yet she couldn't help watching him when he walked across the parking lot, balancing their lunches. He made every other man look like a shadow. Mike's vigilance never relaxed. Even as he walked, he scanned the area.

A warmth stole into her heart. Even if it was his job, no one had ever taken her welfare so to heart. Her father had barely acknowledged her existence, unless dinner wasn't ready when he wanted to eat. Robert sure hadn't had her welfare at heart. Only Mike.

She loved him. It was stupid—futile. Berating herself for being a stupid idiot for falling for him wouldn't change a thing. She loved him.

"You didn't say what you wanted on the burgers, but from the rest of your order, I figured everything," he said as she leaned across and opened his door.

"Absolutely right, thanks."

She took the food, her appetite gone—she wanted instead to feast on Mike. But dutifully she bit into the burger. The taste was amazing, ambrosia. Suddenly she felt ravenous again.

"This is great," she said around the food in her mouth.

Giving a half smile, Mike nodded and bit into his own.

Savannah sat back and savored her lunch. The food on the ranch was wholesome and delicious. But this was junk food heaven. They ate in silence and she enjoyed every morsel. Dipping her French fries into a blob of ketchup at the edge of the paper, she nibbled slowly. It had been months since she'd had such a great lunch.

She and Mike shared the French fries and the onion rings. Once their fingers brushed when they reached at the same time. Savannah watched, timing herself to him. The next time he reached for a fry, her hand was there. For a second, their fingers tangled, held.

Mike's eyes blazed into hers. She felt the heat to her toes. Forgotten was the last bit of hamburger. Her appetite vanished. At least for food. Slowly she let the morsel of bun and meat drop into the paper. Her eyes never moved from his, her mouth opened slightly to better breathe. Would her racing heart burst from her chest?

Mike leaned closer, his hand came up to cup one cheek. His thumb brushed against the corner of her mouth. "You have some mustard here," he said so softly she almost missed the words.

Curling her tongue to the corner of her mouth she licked the spot and touched his thumb.

He groaned and pulled her closer.

"I'll do that," he said, crushing her mouth beneath his.

Savannah grabbed his shoulders and held on as her world tilted and whirled in bright colors and exciting sensations. When his tongue brushed against her lips, she opened her mouth. Wanting to be even closer, she shifted in the narrow seat and moved toward him, ignoring fries, left-over hamburger and drinks.

"What the heck—" Mike reared back and made a frantic grab for his soda which spilled across one jean-clad thigh. "Blast it, that's cold!"

He straightened the cup and grabbed a handful of napkins to blot the liquid.

"Sorry," Savannah said, making an effort to push the rest

of the food out of the way.

Her milkshake had tipped but being so thick hadn't spilled a drop. Using her own napkin, she blotted the damp denim until Mike's hand clamped on her wrist and held her away.

"Don't touch me," he growled.

"I was just trying to help," she protested.

He leaned back against the seat and closed his eyes. "Blast it all. I didn't want this. I only volunteered for the assignment because I knew I could keep a witness safe. I don't need this!"

"Need what?" she asked, confused.

One moment they were kissing like there was no tomorrow and now Mike was complaining.

He rolled his head toward her and glared.

"I don't need this attraction between us," he said slowly through gritted teeth. "You're an assignment, nothing more."

Savannah swiveled around, rolled up to her knees and sank her fists on her hips and glared at him.

"I never asked for any of this, Mr. Almighty U.S. Marshal. In the first place, you could have just said I had something around my mouth and let me take care of it. But, oh, no, you had to take care of it yourself. And as for attraction, it's mutual, or haven't you noticed? And what's the harm? I'm unattached, you're unattached. And maybe I even like it."

A lot!

He looked out the side window. "Stockholm syndrome."

"What?"

"In kidnap or in hostage situations, if the victim falls for their captors, it's called the Stockholm syndrome. That's what you've got. I'm your main contact to the world for the time being. You have to rely on me and only me. So you think you're falling for me. Same as pregnant women fall for their obstetricians."

Savannah stared at him, her mouth dropping. "Are you nuts? I'm not a hostage and I'm not falling in love with you because you're my main contact in life."

"You're not falling in love with me at all," he snapped back, glaring out the window.

"Want to bet?"

When he turned around to look at her, all the heat had vanished. In its place was a chill that shook Savannah.

"Listen to me, Savannah Adams, because I know what I'm talking about. I thought I was in love once with another beautiful woman. Amy Sutcliffe. We were engaged for several months. I was crazy about her. And as a result, my judgment became impaired. She wanted totally different things. She didn't like Denver, yearned for New York. She didn't like my job, wanted me to join her father's company. She wanted bright lights and parties and wild living. But I ignored signs. Then she went on a visit to New York. By the time I caught up with her, the *love* she felt had faded. Gone. Vanished. It didn't end so quickly for me. She found someone else in New York and he was giving her every single thing she asked for."

Savannah sank back on her heels, her gaze never leaving his face.

"I learned a valuable lesson from her. And from my father. I don't want to get entangled with any woman, especially a blond beauty from Miami Beach, who likes bikinis and beach boys and the ocean. Who wouldn't settle in Denver if she was paid to."

Savannah stared at him, her heart dropping. *He'd loved another woman.*

Well, her conscience jeered, so what, you thought you loved Robert. But she'd gotten over Robert.

Mike was different. And the feelings she had were different, stronger, true.

Mike had not gotten over Amy and the hurt she'd inflicted.

"I'm sorry," she whispered.

He looked down at his jeans, at the soggy, wadded napkins in his hand and shrugged.

"Time heals most things. I learned an important lesson. No matter how attracted I am to you, or you to me, it'll fade a week after you're home."

She sat back and crumbled the paper holding the remainder of her hamburger into a ball, dropping it into the bag of trash. Taking her milkshake, she tried to keep the words from echoing in her mind. She didn't think she'd get over him in a week.

The chocolate tasted like sawdust in her mouth. Breathing slowly, deeply, she tried to keep the tears at bay. Suddenly, she was tired. She wanted to get her own life back!

She'd give anything to turn back the clock and stay home that fateful night.

Would she really?

That'd mean she'd never have met Mike Black. And despite the heartache that waited, she was glad she had. Savannah knew she'd miss him when she returned to Miami. She might always long for something that never could be.

But right now she had a few more days, a few more hours with him, time to build up memories to tide her over the empty years ahead.

The awkward silence stretched out endlessly. Finally Savannah slurped the last of her milkshake and dropped the cup into the bag. As if waiting for a signal, Mike grabbed the trash and opened his door.

Maybe he needed the time and distance it took to throw it into the trash can. Savannah watched him until he turned around, then deliberately looked away. She wouldn't give him any more ammunition to scar her already wounded heart.

"Where to now?" she asked brightly when he once again joined her in the Jeep.

"We'll hit the shops like you want. But don't take all afternoon."

"I can't imagine Laramie has that many women's boutiques. What movie do you want to see?"

Savannah refused to open herself up to anything more from Mike Black. When they walked down First Street, she kept her distance. When passing other pedestrians, Mike drew protectively near. She never let him touch her. Sidestepping, she kept a zone around herself that she wouldn't let him cross.

Her enjoyment of the afternoon dimmed after the confrontation at lunch. Instead she came up with a dozen questions about Amy Sutcliffe. What had she been like. How had they met? What had he expected in a marriage? Was he still a bit in love with her? What if he were wrong and Savannah didn't get over him in a week?

"That's it. I've seen enough," she said after browsing a dozen stores on First and Second Streets. "I'm ready for the movies and popcorn."

"You want to eat again? You just had lunch."

"One does not go to the show without popcorn and a soda," Savannah said as if stating a sacred principle.

"The movie house is near the campus."

"Lead on, Marshal."

When they reached the multi-theater movie complex, Savannah studied the listings. "I don't want to see blood and gore," she said firmly. She'd had enough of that in real life to last a long time.

"I don't want to see that sappy romantic one," he quickly returned.

She shook her head, "I don't, either."

It'd be too painful to watch someone fall in love and end up happily ever after when her own life never seemed headed in that direction.

"How about the comedy?"

"Fine."

Mike welcomed the movie. It'd give him a couple hours downtime.

He knew Savannah was hurt from what he'd said earlier and he wished he hadn't been so blunt. But there was no use in pretending things were any different from what they were. No matter how much he wanted to be with her, he knew once she returned to her normal routine, he'd be nothing but a painful memory of a bad period in her life.

After the movie, he'd find a quiet place for dinner and then head for home.

It only seemed like the day was lasting forever. In a few hours, she'd go to bed and he'd be alone.

The way he liked it.

Savannah had trouble focusing on the movie. What would Mike think if she moved one seat over to her left and kept an empty one between them? He'd probably think she was pouting.

She wasn't, but sitting so close she could feel his body heat wasn't helping her concentrate on the movie. His arm leaned on the armrest between them, and she hunched over toward her left, as far away from his disturbing proximity as she could get. She'd insisted on separate bags of popcorn, refusing to allow her fingers tangled with his again.

But hovering over all was the burning hurt he'd inflicted by his casual dismissal of her declaration of love.

Her emotions were not some stupid syndrome.

She'd been guarded by marshals for the last several months. She'd never felt a flicker of the emotion with any of the others.

And she didn't even like him all the time. When he acted like a general, she wanted to slap him down.

But she loved him. She relished the time they shared. She liked looking at him and teasing him. And kissing him. And nothing he said would change that for a long, long time.

Not that she'd ever tell him again. If he thought her love was a temporary aberration as a result of their close proximity, she'd let it lie there.

The last thing she wanted was for him to feel any kind of pity for her. So she had a history of falling for the wrong man. Maybe one day she'd get it right. Or maybe not.

But she'd never let him know how important he'd become to her.

When the audience laughed, she brought her attention back to the screen. She needed to pay attention, to forget the ache in her heart and focus on the present, not what might have been.

She was lucky to have her life. Lucky to have met Mike. It'd have to be enough.

Savannah fulfilled Mike's every expectation of a ditzy blonde at dinner. She flirted with him, with the waiter, even with one of the other patrons who waited in the lobby with them.

She told nonsensical tales about Miami Beach, about the Latin Lovers that roamed the beaches looking for snowbirds who came south with romance in mind.

She told him outrageous stories about her early days working in the boutique. She made him laugh, and frown, and was satisfied that he watched her carefully the entire time.

She fooled him into thinking she was carefree and happy. Never for a moment did he guess how much she wanted to go home, climb into bed and cry her eyes out.

"Ready to leave?" he asked when she set her coffee cup down.

"To go to the country-western bar?" she asked brightly.

"Home."

"I thought we were going to join some of the cowboys from the ranch at the O.K. Corral."

"No."

"Why not?"

Anger began to build, but she clamped down on it. First, find out what he had in mind. Then explode.

"Savannah, we came today to get you away from the ranch. You've had your day, it's time to head home."

"The last I heard you thought the men after me believed

I'm still in Florida. No one around here has given you a reason to suspect there's any danger. I want to go dancing!"

He leaned over the table and glared at her.

"Is that all you think about, good times? We came out today so you could enjoy yourself. Your life is in danger. I'm doing what I think best to keep you safe. That puts my life in danger, as well. But don't think about that, Ms. Adams, think about your own good time!"

"Good time? *Good time?* My life's in shambles. I haven't been home in months. I may not have a job anymore. I'm scared to death half my waking hours. I have nightmares so bad I can't sleep most nights. And you think I'm worried about a good time! You are absolutely nuts! I'm trying my best to keep a cheerful demeanor in the face of all that's gone wrong in my life, through no fault of my own. I won't be a burden on other people, nor make them constantly aware of the fears I'm living with, but good times have nothing to do with anything. I wanted to go dancing for a few hours to try to forget this threat that hangs over me. If that's a crime, then I'm guilty."

She tossed her napkin on the plate and shoved back her chair. Tears threatened to spill down her cheeks as she spun around and stormed toward the back of the restaurant searching for the ladies rest rooms.

Mike watched her stomp away, knowing he'd been off base. Of course she had to be scared. Twice someone tried to kill her and come close if the reports were accurate.

She was living two thousand miles from home and friends. Her life had been disrupted for over six months because she'd witnessed a major crime. And he berated her as if she were guilty of the crime.

He watched the rest room door, waiting. He knew about the nightmares. Hadn't he comforted her a time or two? But he hadn't thought that her bright and cheery demeanor camouflage terror.

He'd taken her at face value not suspecting for a moment that it was an act.

So much for his intuition and detective skills.

The minutes ticked by. Mike wondered if he'd have to send a waitress in after her when she finally came out.

He tossed some bills on the table and intercepted her. "Let's go. Trevor and Steve will be wondering where we are."

"So this is a country-western bar," Savannah said when they arrived at the O.K. Corral ten minutes later. Neither said a word on the ride over.

Savannah was still upset at his accusation. She didn't know why he'd changed his mind, but she was glad he had. Wood paneling covered the walls. A huge mirror hung behind the old-fashioned bar. The place consisted of one large room, with another in back through an arch. Wooden tables and chairs were scattered around the room. In one corner a small band, containing a couple of guitarists, a drummer and piano player, tuned up. In front of them was a dance floor.

"Never been in one before?" Mike asked, scanning the area, making sure nothing looked out of place. Gradually he relaxed. He recognized several of the patrons. Savannah was right. No one suspected she was hidden in Wyoming.

They found a couple of chairs at an empty table and sat, but when the music started, Savannah was asked to dance by a tall rancher, wearing the ubiquitous jeans, boots and Stetson. He introduced himself as Rusty Morgan.

She glanced to Mike, wondering if he'd say no. He shrugged and nodded, though his eyes narrowed.

"New in town, darlin'?" Rusty asked as they began to move to the lively music.

"Just visiting at the Bar B," she replied, trying to match steps in a dance she was totally unfamiliar with.

"Friend of Sarah?" he asked, twirling her around.

"Mike," she said when she could catch her breath.

"Didn't think he was much for the ladies," Rusty said.

"He doesn't have to be much for the ladies. We're only friends."

Maybe not even that, she thought sadly.

"If you're just friends, you can see other men."

She looked up at him and smiled. "I sure can, sugar, but I'm a bit selective."

The music changed tempo and segued into a slow ballad. Rusty pulled her closer.

"I'm a mite selective myself," he said, dropping his head until his cheek rested against her hair. "Where're you from, little darlin'? Your accent's so thick I could cut it."

"Florida. Ever been to Miami Beach?"

"Never. But I could be talked into a visit."

She giggled. Now this was first class flirting. Mike should hear this, then he'd know she hadn't been flirting at the ranch.

"Want to slip away for a drink or two? I know a quieter bar not too far away." he asked as they moved slowly to the music's dreamy beat. She wished for a moment that Mike had asked her dance. She wouldn't mind being held in his arms.

But Rusty was the one holding her, and a bit too tightly, to say the least.

"Now, Rusty, that just wouldn't be polite. After all, Mike brought me here. I ought to go home with him, don't you think?"

Rusty looked up, located Mike and grinned.

"Now, darlin', that cowboy looks plumb fit to be tied. I think you'd be safer going home with me." He looked down into her eyes and smiled.

Savannah smiled back. He was fun. Her heart didn't skip a single beat and for the first time in a long time she let go and enjoyed herself. Mike would keep her safe. He didn't want her for himself, so maybe she should flirt with whomever she wanted and enjoy the evening. In only a couple of days she'd be on her way back to Miami.

"I don't know many cowboys, but are they all as fast as you?" she asked.

"Honey, if I don't cut you from the herd quick, there's no telling how many cowboys you'll meet up with. But I know a prize when I see it. We'll have a drink and you can tell me the story of your life." He nuzzled her neck.

"And when do you tell me yours?"

"Any time. Later tonight, if you like. All night long, if you like. Or at breakfast?"

Before she could think of a sassy response to his teasing, Mike's firm hand gripped her upper arm and pulled her away from Rusty.

"You've run out of time, Savannah. Say good-night to Rusty."

"Hey, man, the lady and I were still dancing," Rusty protested.

"Mike, let me go!"

Savannah flushed with embarrassment.

"Did Savannah tell you we were engaged?" Mike asked.

Rusty looked surprised. "No. She didn't mention it. Said you two were friends. Didn't mean to take your girl, Mike."

"We were just dancing, Mike, don't make a federal case out of it. And I'm not sure we're even friends!"

She snatched her arm free and turned back to Rusty. "Thank you for the dance and the conversation. I enjoyed myself."

With a glare at Mike, she stalked off the floor and headed for the ladies' room. It seemed the place of choice tonight. She'd have done better to just go back to the ranch.

Her privacy was short-lived. Five minutes later one of the other women whom Savannah had seen dancing came in. She smiled at Savannah.

"Hi."

"Hi," Savannah said, wondering how long she could stay away from Mike. He made her so angry.

"You're with Mike Black, aren't you? He's outside looking like he could chew nails."

"He looks like that a lot," Savannah said.

"Congratulations on getting engaged. He's never been with anyone special before."

"It may be the world's shortest engagement," she mumbled.

"Well, you've got to expect a man to be jealous when his woman's dancing with the town's more notorious lady-killer and seems to be enjoying it."

"Rusty?" Savannah asked incredulously, her gaze meeting the other woman's.

"Sure. He can charm the birds from the trees and has broken more than one heart on the dance floor."

"He was being nice."

The other woman laughed softly. "Right. My guess is you couldn't even see him for Mike. Which would make Mike a lucky man. Go cheer him up, honey."

Savannah smiled and headed for the door, feeling as if she were heading for her execution. She was the last person able to cheer Mike up. He probably wished, and not for the first time, that he'd never brought her into Laramie today.

"Ready to leave?" he asked as soon as she left the ladies' room.

"No, I'm not. I came to dance and I want to dance. I see Hank and Steve. If you want to go home, go. They can bring me later."

She refused to shorten her one day of freedom in months.

"Fine, we'll dance."

His grip on her hand hurt, but she was so startled at his pronouncement, she could only stumble after him.

Dance they did. Every song the band played Mike danced with her. His eyes glittered as if challenging her to say stop. Hers flashed back—never.

She was unfamiliar with the two-step, he taught her. Unfamiliar with the songs, she soon caught on to the rhythm.

When the slow melodies drifted down, she found herself caught up in a tight embrace as Mike held her so close it was difficult to move without every inch of her body brushing against his.

Her head swam, her senses reeled. Wrapped in his arms, she ignored the coldness in his expression and imagine he wanted her as close as she wanted to be. Could pretend he loved her like he'd once loved Amy.

Could dream he loved her as she loved him.

Nine

Savannah and Mike bumped into Rusty a time or two. He'd grin and give her a wink. She smiled in recognition at the woman who had spoken to her earlier when the dance brought them closer.

Conversations were impossible.

She saw the other cowboys from the ranch and waved, feeling a part of the group when they brought some more chairs and squeezed in at their table to sit out a song now and then. She wondered at one point in the evening if Miami had anything like it. There were cattle ranches in Florida. Did those cowboys kick up as much fun as this group? Maybe she'd try one and see.

But in the back of her mind, she knew she wouldn't. Visiting a cowboy bar in Florida would only remind her of tonight.

Her enjoyment of the evening diminished slightly by Mike's brooding presence, his eyes ever scanning the room, his attention fully on her, but not as a beloved fiancé as most of the cowboys teased, but as a marshal with his assignment.

The band announced another ballad before taking a break. Steve smiled and started to draw Savannah into his arms when Mike stepped up.

"This one's mine."

Savannah went willingly into his arms. He pulled her closer than necessary, but she didn't object. Closing her eyes, she snuggled as the sad tune drifted across the room. She could stay like this all night—slow dancing with Mike. Ever mindful of his cutting words at lunch, his slashing anger at dinner, she tried to block them, tried to enjoy the moment, knowing full well when the evening ended, her dreams would end forever.

His breath fanned across her cheek, his hands spread across her back, holding her as if she were a precious porcelain figurine.

"Thank you for bringing me into town today," she said softly. "I was glad to get out for a while."

"Not as much excitement in Laramie as in Miami," he murmured as they swayed to the music.

"Maybe there's excitement in Miami, but I've missed it—unless you count watching one man murder another. Usually I live a fairly routine life. I enjoyed seeing where you went to college, seeing the different shops on First Street."

"And how many new ideas did you get for your own shop?" he asked.

"A few."

If she still had a job. Again the uncertainties rose. It wouldn't be long before all her questions were answered. They were heading back in a couple of days.

Two days left on the Bar B.

Two days left to spend with Mike.

She stumbled and pulled back.

"I think I want to go home now."

Turning without waiting to see his reaction, she headed

for the front door.

Several people called good-bye and she waved, trying to smile, wondering if it appeared a mere caricature. She didn't feel in the least like smiling.

"Wait a moment."

Mike caught her at the door. He took her arm and led the way, pausing only a moment to scan the parking lot.

"The thing I won't miss is constantly searching every nook and cranny for possible men with guns," she murmured as they hurried to the Jeep.

"Every indication we have is they think you're still in Florida. Still, I'd be remiss if I didn't check."

She looked at Mike in the faint light. He looked strong and vigilant. The kind of man she never dated, never interested. Was it any wonder he showed no interest in her now?

She wished she hadn't said anything earlier. Wished she could have lived her fantasy for a little longer. Wished she could have at least held on to the hope that one day he might fall in love with her.

She loved him and he didn't even believe her.

So be it. She swallowed hard, determined to get through the next few days with her pride intact. When he pulled out onto the street, she turned slightly.

"What will you do when this assignment is finished?" she asked.

She'd gather every speck of information she could. Then when she thought about him in the future, she could imagine what he was doing, where he lived, how he felt about things. Even though they wouldn't be together, she'd know that somewhere in the world Mike Black was alive and well.

166

It'd have to be enough, it was all she'd get.

"Get another one."

"Guarding another witness?"

"Another assignment. Don't know what. Transporting a prisoner, investigating a drug ring. Providing security for visiting heads of state."

"When does that happen?"

"Colorado has some amazing ski resorts visited by people from all over the world. You'd be surprised who shows up now and then."

"If I'm the only witness you've brought to the Bar B, where do you usually go if you're guarding someone?"

"The marshal's service has safe houses in Denver. We thought at first there might have been a leak in the department, but since the second incident in Miami, we're leaning more toward the fact that they found you before was coincidence."

"So we could have stayed at one of the safe houses in Denver?"

"You probably would have been safe in a different safe house in Florida," he said.

And we never would have met.

She wondered for a moment if it would have been better to live her life never knowing Mike. She wouldn't have this ache in her heart.

But neither would she have the memories to cherish. Nor the explosion of passion that he caused. At least she'd had that once. She knew now she would refuse to settle for anything less in the future.

"Do you have an apartment in Denver or a house?"

"What is this, twenty questions?" he asked.

"I'm just making conversation. You could volunteer something so I don't have to drag everything out of you. Make some conversation yourself then."

"All right, the weather is usual for this time of year. We rarely get a lot of rain, just the occasional thunderstorm. I think the price of beef is going to hold through the sale, which will make a tidy profit for the Bar B. Tom and Sarah will be home soon, so we need to do some laundry tomorrow."

She stared out of the side window, her eyes shimmering with unshed tears. Not one word he spoke could be considered personal. It seemed as if he erected a huge No Trespassing sign. When a lonely tear spilled over, she reached up slowly to brush it from her cheek.

"Darn it, Savannah, if you're crying I'll—"

"You'll what?" she asked, keeping her face averted. One tear didn't mean she was crying.

"I don't know. Just don't cry."

"I'm not. I had something in my eye. Why would I cry anyway? I had a good time today, most of today. I enjoyed the dancing. Steve is quite something when he—"

"I don't want to hear about Steve. Or Rusty. Or any of the other cowboys."

"Why, Marshal, you sound almost jealous. I thought you'd be glad to see I had other interests beside you," she mocked.

"I'm not jealous," he snapped.

"Could have fooled me," she murmured.

"We're playing a charade. You blew it tonight flirting with Rusty."

"No. I didn't. I enjoyed myself and had a good time.

Everyone there was having a good time. No one made lasting commitments." Least of all you.

Mike remained silent for the rest of the ride to the ranch. Savannah wondered at the note she'd detected in his tone. Could he possibly be jealous? Could he care for her more than he felt he should? Was he pushing her away because of *duty*?

The porch light was on and lights shone from the bunkhouse. Of course, Savannah thought, someone had to stay at the ranch in case of an emergency. She wondered who'd stayed home.

She waited by the front door while Mike made a quick sweep through the house. When he flicked on the lights, she knew it was safe to enter. She headed for the kitchen. She wanted something to drink before bed. Something to help her unwind.

"Hungry?" Mike stood in the doorway as she rummaged through the cabinets.

"No. Ah, here it is. I thought there'd be some. I wanted some hot cocoa before bed, want some?"

"I'd rather have a beer."

"There's some in the refrigerator."

She pulled out a bottle and held it out for him. When he took it, she turned quickly back to retrieve the milk. Glad to have something to occupy her attention, she turned to the stove. She'd prepare her drink and get to her room.

There was a decidedly homey feel to being in the kitchen late at night together—almost like playing house.

Savannah became aware of Mike's every move. From the tilting of the long-neck bottle to his lips, to the rhythmic movement in his throat when he swallowed. Her fingers tingled with yearning to touch him, to feel his taut skin, to trace his throat, down to the broad expanse of his chest.

If she kissed him now, he'd taste of beer and male heat. She shivered slightly and stirred the milk faithfully. The idea of the cocoa was to soothe her so she could sleep.

Images of touching Mike would keep her up all night!

"Savannah."

"What?" She blinked and looked up.

"Your milk's boiling."

She looked at the pan, sure enough the milk boiled and bubbled. She pulled it from the burner and turned off the flame. Dumping in the cocoa, she stirred vigorously, wishing he'd leave.

How was a woman to do anything when he stood so close? She'd totally lost concentration, too busy thinking about his mouth on hers, his hands caressing her, the sensations that his touch sparked.

"I don't know what you're doing, but that cocoa has been beat to death."

His warm hand covered hers and stopped her stirring.

She stepped back, right into the hard wall of his chest. Warmth enveloped her. For a moment Savannah didn't want to move—she could stand here forever, with Mike behind her, one arm almost around her.

"I was just mixing it enough to make sure there were no undissolved—"

"It's mixed." He turned her to face him. His eyes held the same heat she'd seen earlier.

"Mike, what if you're wrong?" she blurted out.

"It is mixed, I've been watching you, there's no way—"

"No, not the cocoa, about us, I mean. About this

attraction between us. What if you're wrong? What if we are meant to be together? Shouldn't we explore it a bit more? I'm sorry about your experience with Amy, but you and me may be different. I didn't feel this way about the other marshals."

She'd never felt this way before, not even Robert. She loved this hardheaded man.

Why couldn't he at least acknowledge the possibility of something between them and see where they'd end up? Or would he never trust again after Amy?

His hands cupped her jaw, his fingers spearing into her soft hair. "We can explore this sexual pull of attraction all you want, but it won't change anything. In two days you go home. A week or two after the trial, you'll have forgotten all about this."

Savannah stood on tiptoes and brushed her lips against his.

"I don't think I'll ever forget a minute of this, Marshal Black."

He hesitated a split second then with a sigh gave in and covered her lips with his own. His hands tilted her face to give him better access and he deepened the kiss until Savannah felt as if she floated. There was no earth or sky or sea, only the heaven of his embrace.

His warm palms cradled her jaw, his fingers moved in her hair. His lips felt warm and firm and moved with a master's touch. When his tongue brushed against the seam of her lips, she parted them, welcoming his sweet invasion Her heart skipped a beat, then raced as her blood carried the heated message to every cell.

When his hands moved to her back, pressing her against

his length, she tried to snuggle even closer. She wanted more. His kisses inflamed her, she needed more to quench the fire.

His hair was thick and silky to her touch. She tangled her fingers in it and held his head closer. She rubbed herself against him like a kitten seeking affection.

Her senses spun when he picked her up in his arms and headed for her room.

She flung her arms around his neck and held on, her heart racing, blood thundering in her veins. His taut muscles held her easily, proving his strength. She had never felt so cherished as this by such a romantic move.

He was going to make love to her! He couldn't resist the attraction any more than she could. And he'd discover how deep her love was, how strong. She'd show him in every way. Rising excitement drowned the lingering apprehension. She loved him. And she was convinced he cared something for her. He didn't see her as solely an assignment. In time wouldn't he grow to love her as much as she loved him?

When he reached her room, Mike didn't turn on the light, but found his way to her bed by the light spilling in from the living room. Stars shone through the open window, giving the room a romantic ambiance. Slowly he let her feet down, let her body slip down his until she stood, her arms still locked around his neck. Every inch burned where she touched his hard body. Butterflies danced in her stomach, her legs felt as shaky as jelly. She lifted her head for another kiss.

"You would tempt a saint, Savannah, and I'm no saint. But I am a man who does his job to the best of his ability. If you want to stay safe another two days, stop playing your flirtatious games with me."

He kissed her hard then left, slamming the door behind him.

Stunned, Savannah collapsed back onto her bed

He wanted her, she knew that. She wanted him. She'd been more than clear with her kisses and caresses.

But it wasn't enough. It had never been enough!

"You only have to tell me two or three times, before I get it, I guess," she murmured slowly, feeling like a total idiot.

Numb with shock, she rose and dressed for bed. Slipping beneath the covers, she pulled them over her head, wishing she could shut out her thoughts as easily as she shut out the night sky. A man couldn't make it any clearer than Mike had done.

He was not interested.

For the next two days, Savannah avoided Mike. She kept to her room if he was in the house. Mike tried once to get her to join him in a ride and she pleaded a headache.

When she refused to go to dinner at the bunk house one night, he'd barged in and told her to quit sulking and come eat. She'd ignored him and turned her back.

"I have a migraine headache. Light, noise and food all make me sick," she'd said.

But when she knew he was otherwise occupied, she wandered to the barn to watch the cowboys work and soak up memories.

She'd grown to like Wyoming. It would always be vastly different from Miami, and she missed the beach, but over the weeks the beauty and agelessness of the ranch had seeped into her until she grew almost comfortable being here.

Horses hadn't proved the wonder she'd thought they were when she was a teenager. Still, she enjoyed riding.

She'd been thrilled to watch Mike ride the wild horse. She'd learned so much when he took her out on the range.

And she was still charmed with the camaraderie that was so evident on the ranch. Wistfully, she wondered if she could ever come back.

The day they were to travel to Florida, Savannah rose early, dressed and folded the few articles of clothing she'd acquired. She had no suitcase. Did the marshal's service mean for her to keep the clothes? Or was she to leave them behind?

She left them on the dresser.

It was hard to believe that tonight she'd be home. She could hardly wait. It'd been over six months since she'd gone out late one night for ice cream. Nothing had been the same since. Soon she'd be home and in a few days be able to pick up the pieces of her life.

It proved harder than she had expected to say good-bye to the cowboys. Jason made her sandwiches and cookies to take with her. She gave him a hug and kissed his cheek.

"Airport food's no good," he mumbled at her thanks.

"And the coffee will seem so bland," she murmured.

"Thought you'd like a rodeo poster," Steve said, giving her a rolled up poster.

She smiled and nodded. "I would. Thanks."

Each of the men had something special to say or a small gift.

She smiled and laughed and joked with them as if she

were the carefree girl she'd never been.

Mike watched, his frown growing with each hug, each cheek kissed until the last man had made his farewell. Then he hustled her to the Jeep.

Heading toward the highway, Savannah kept her smile firmly in place. Her eyes drank in every inch of the Bar B, committing it to memory. Would she ever see another ranch to compare it to? Would she ever talk to a cowboy and not remember the men of the Bar B?

"You'll be back in Florida before bedtime," Mike said as they turned toward Denver.

"Good. Will I get to stay at my house?"

"No. We've taken a couple of rooms at a hotel. One of our female field officers will have some of your clothes there. The jury's been selected, the testimony part of the trial starts tomorrow. You'll have a phalanx of guards. Once you testify, the threat will be null. Word on the street is that Ramirez's contract is only to stop you from testifying. We don't count on a revenge angle. Once you've talked, the damage is done. He's a man to cut his losses and concentrate on the main deal. He'll need his money to fight the verdict, not have you killed."

"I hope you're right."

"We wouldn't let you go if we thought differently."

She wanted to ask if he planned to stay until the trial ended, but couldn't say the words. And it really didn't matter.

He'd made his position perfectly clear two nights ago.

She'd never reveal how her heart ached, nor how she wanted to rail at fate for its capriciousness. Maybe it was her destiny to go through life alone. She should stop looking for a man to share it with her.

The scenery on the drive to Denver was spectacular. Savannah missed it three weeks ago and gazed avidly from the window the entire trip. Once on the plane, Savannah asked for headphones. She listened to music and ignored the man sitting so close. She only had another few hours until she could be alone again. She'd make it. She'd endured the last several months, and was still alive and kicking.

She'd survive another love gone wrong.

After changing planes once, they arrived in Miami late at night. Immediately after stepping from the plane, Savannah knew she was home. The air had the tang of salt she loved. The warm humid southern air moved in balmy waves across her skin. In only a few moments, they were whisked away into a dark car, surrounded by men in dark suits with alert, ever scanning eyes.

The bright lights and the crowded streets seemed alien after several weeks in the dark emptiness of Wyoming. Savannah avidly took in the brightly lit high-rises along the beach, the garish neon lights flashing along the street advertising bars and restaurants and movie theaters. People crowded the sidewalks wearing shorts and bathing suits and flashy sun dresses. She was home.

When they reached the hotel, Savannah was met at the door of the suite by a female agent.

"Hi, welcome back to Miami. I'm Alicia Longstreet."

The marshal held up her identification giving Savannah time to examine it.

"Thanks, guys, I'll take it from here."

Alicia smiled at the three men in the hallway and calmly closed the door in their faces.

Savannah looked around. She hadn't had a chance to tell

Mike good-bye.

"Are you my new bodyguard?" she asked.

"For the duration of the trial I'll be with you every step of the way."

"What about Marshal Black?"

"We don't want you alone even in the rest rooms. I hear Black's good, but he can't go where I can." Alicia smiled and waved her hand around the room. "Nice, don't you think? I picked up a bunch of things from your house last week. We didn't want to give anyone a lead, so I've been changing hotels and hiding out to throw anyone off our trail. Of course they all know where you'll be at ten o'clock tomorrow. But we'll have you covered."

"And Marshal Black?"

Was that it? Was he leaving now that the Miami office was back in charge? Didn't she even get a chance to tell him good-bye?

Alicia stepped closer and studied Savannah for a moment.

"I imagine he'll go back to Colorado and get his next assignment."

"No. I want him here until the trial is over," Savannah said firmly, damping down the rising panic. "Call whoever you have to, but he stays with me."

"I can guard you," Alicia said evenly.

"Maybe, but I trust Mike Black. I want him here."

It didn't matter that she sounded like a spoiled petulant child. She'd been through a lot to stay alive to testify for the prosecution. The least they could do was accommodate her wishes.

She was afraid Mike would disappear before she got to

see him again. Surely it wouldn't hurt things to have him with her through the trial.

"I'll check in with headquarters and pass along your request," Alicia said, moving toward the phone. "Meantime, I'm here and you're safe. Want to take a bath?"

"That sounds heavenly!"

"Through that door, the room has two beds, we'll be sharing."

"Fine."

Savannah went through the door to the left and entered the bedroom. The two queen-size beds occupied a good portion of the room. She went to the closet and opened it. A row of familiar dresses and suits hung from the rod. Smiling, she reached out to touch them. She turned to the dresser and opened a drawer—underwear, stockings and a nightie, all folded neatly. Grabbing a fresh change, she headed for the bathroom.

She soaked for almost an hour, luxuriating in the warm water scented with bath oil. The bathroom was almost as large as the bedroom, with a huge tub, shower, even a phone on the wall. Dressed in a familiar nightgown, she brushed her hair and went back to the bedroom.

Alicia lay on one of the beds, reading a magazine. She looked up when Savannah entered.

"Your every wish is our command, madam. Mike Black will be in the group picking us up tomorrow to take us to the courthouse. He'll be with you until the marshal's service determines there's no longer a threat to your safety."

Savannah smiled.

"Thanks. What are you reading? I haven't seen a

magazine since the safe house, before the one that blew up."

There were certain things a female agent was better at, she thought when Alicia tossed her a couple of women's magazines.

And tomorrow, she'd see Mike again.

The next morning Savannah took great pains in dressing. She wore an electric blue suit with a snowy-white blouse. The short sassy skirt showed her shapely, tanned legs to great advantage. She applied makeup Alicia had brought, satisfied with the effect she made. Her eyes appeared a deeper blue. Her hair waved softly around her face. Checking herself out in the mirror, she smiled.

"Eat your heart out, Marshal," she said softly.

Maybe his will was as strong as he thought, but she saw no reason he shouldn't regret it a bit.

She entered the living room of the suite as the knock came on the door. Alicia checked through the peephole and then opened the door.

Mike and two other men entered.

For a moment Savannah almost didn't recognize him. His hair was cut short. His dark suit and power red tie matched the other men. His stern look and scanning eyes marked him as the powerful, dedicated law enforcement officer he was.

He looked good enough to eat. She couldn't see the others for Mike. His jaw was freshly shaved, and she longed to feel the softness of his skin over the rock-hard jawbone. His eyes sought hers, held. She felt the heat that flashed between them.

"Ready?" he asked.

She smiled and nodded. "As I'll ever be. Let's go put some bad guys away."

Mike stepped into the hall and glanced around. He needed the break. His eyes would pop out of his head if he had to watch Savannah sashay across the room in that indecently short skirt. Her legs were curvy and sexy and she had to know she was raising the blood pressure of every man in sight with the snug-fitting skirt and jacket. And the white loose blousey thing she had on draped over her shapely breasts like a lover.

He wanted to order the other marshals to look away, but couldn't blame them for being taken in by her sultry smile and provocative walk. Wait until she began to flirt with them—they wouldn't know what hit them.

When Savannah stepped into the hall, he took her arm. He could no more let her pass by without touching her than he could stop breathing.

She looked up in surprise. Was it his imagination or were her eyes so blue he could drown in them? Her lips were rosy, soft and moist. He almost gave in to the craving to lean forward and brush his across them one last time.

He thought he'd be on his way back to Colorado by now, but the Florida office had asked him to stay. He should have refused, knew he couldn't.

When they reached the dark sedan, Alicia climbed into the front with Sam Timms, the marshal who'd drive. Mike held a back door for Savannah and sat down beside her. The other marshal entered from the opposite door.

Mike had barely settled before Savannah scooted closer. Her leg brushed his. Involuntarily, he reached out and yanked on her skirt, trying to cover another inch or two of silk clad thigh. His fingers burned where they touched her. Snatching his hand away, he glared out the window.

Savannah felt as if her leg were on fire from the touch of Mike's fingers. She looked at him from beneath her lashes. He wasn't immune to her, she knew that. And she certainly wasn't feeling immune, either. She wanted to fling herself into his arms and demand he love her.

Oh, sure, he'd do that. And maybe Wyoming would become beach-front property.

"Nervous?" Mike asked as she fidgeted at his side.

"A little." She hesitated a minute then smiled shyly. "Actually I think I'm scared to death."

His hand covered hers, solid and strong. "We won't let anyone harm you, Savannah."

Letting the reassurance flow through her, she tried to relax.

She wished he'd continue to keep her safe after the trial.

Ten

Savannah entered the courthouse through the back entrance. Alicia stuck as close as glue, with Mike right behind her. Nervously Savannah gazed around to see if she could spot anyone who looked threatening.

At each entrance uniformed policemen stood and she felt almost as safe as she had on the ranch. She was reasonably certain these marshals would do everything to protect her.

As they passed the courtroom, Savannah saw it was packed. She was taken to a small ante room off the main hall.

"We'll be here until you're called," Alice said.

Savannah was thankful for the privacy. She wanted to give her testimony and leave. Once she'd reported what she'd seen, Ramirez would have no further reason to eliminate her—unless for revenge. No one seemed to feel he'd spend that kind of money on revenge. She hoped they were right.

An assistant district attorney came in to discuss her testimony. They had gone over the procedure months ago, so Savannah felt this was a refresher course that she aced.

The morning dragged by after that. One of the marshals popped his head in periodically to report what was happening. Preliminary remarks were made.

An hour later he reported the first policemen on the scene were giving testimony.

Savannah wanted to cut through the routine so she could testify. Tension built as the day progressed. What if they didn't call her today? What if she had to go through this all over again tomorrow?

Lunch was brought in.

"Great—hamburgers! You know, I stayed three weeks at a cattle ranch in Wyoming and we ate almost every cut of beef there is, but I only had hamburgers once," she said, smiling at Alicia, throwing a teasing grin at Mike. Instantly she remembered their lunch—and the way he'd kissed her.

She looked away, her natural exuberance dimmed.

Suddenly the hamburger tasted like sawdust. She forced it down so no one would notice, and tried to push away the memories of a certain lunch in Laramie.

Concentrating on the easy talk among the marshals, she tried to forget the reason they surrounded her. Soon things would be back to normal. She clung to the idea even as she tried to ignore the fact Mike would leave when that time arrived.

"You're next," the marshal said mid afternoon.

She took a deep breath. Show time. She looked at Mike.

"You're going to do great. Just remember things the way they were. And don't look at Ramirez. Focus on the attorney asking the questions," Mike said softly in her ear.

Mike smiled and Savannah's heart flipped over. That adorable dimple. She was no more immune to it now that she'd been upon first seeing it. Slowly she raised her gaze to lock with his, hoping he couldn't see how his smile dazzled her.

"If they ask you to point him out, like the DA said, look at his jaw or ear, but not into his eyes, and only when you have to. Your testimony will put him away, Savannah. He won't be a threat much longer."

"Do you think I'll get to the stand today?" she asked.

Mike shrugged. If the judge didn't call an early adjournment, she could get started today. It might be several days before the attorneys finished questioning her on all she recalled.

He wouldn't tell her that. Her nerves were already stretched tight. He glanced at her and saw a poised, confident young woman. Only he knew she practically seethed with tension.

Glancing beyond her, he saw Alicia on the alert. Why had he been asked to remain in Florida? There were good officers in the Miami office, he wasn't needed.

Unless Savannah had asked for him. Granted it gave him a few more days with her. When the danger passed, he'd return to Colorado and Savannah would return to her life in Miami.

Any emotions she attributed to love would fade once she resumed her regular routine. And the feelings he clamped down on would fade as well. He'd learned that much from Amy. Only this time there wouldn't be the heartache, the aching need that he'd experienced before. He'd make sure of that!

"The first thing I'm going to do when this is over is spend a day at the beach," she said walking out of the anteroom and into the spacious hall. A uniformed officer opened the door to the courtroom.

She saw a sea of faces as everyone looked back to see who was coming in. Grateful for Mike's hand at the small of her back, she raised her head and caught the gaze of the district attorney. Clinging to that, she walked forward and to the witness chair when he indicated it.

She sought Mike when she sat down and saw him at the back of the room. She gave him a smile and hoped no one knew how scared she was.

The district attorney began his questions. He started with ones she only had to answer yes or no to.

The judge stopped him at one point asking how much longer he might be. When told a while, the judge recessed until the next morning.

Savannah had never looked at Ramirez, though she could see him from the corner of her eye. She looked at Mike when the judge banged the gavel.

She had to come back again!

She hadn't counted on that. And so far she really hadn't said anything that would convict the murderer.

She and Alicia returned to the hotel and ordered dinner from room service. Listless and tired after being keyed up all day, and then disappointed in how short a time she'd been on the witness stand, Savannah went to bed early.

In the middle of the night she awoke, screaming. Alicia woke instantly, switching on the lamp flooding the room with light. She'd jumped up from her bed gun in hand and slowly scanned the room.

Savannah shook her head as she came fully awake, feeling the fleeting tendrils of terror fading in the bright bedroom light.

"I'm so sorry, Alicia." She shivered, remembering the terror.

Alicia sat on the edge of her mattress and patted her shoulder. "Are you all right? I thought someone was being murdered."

"Yes, I'm fine. Or I will be soon."

Savannah wished Mike sat beside her instead of Alicia. He would draw her into his arms and hold her tightly until the fear receded. She missed that. Missed him. She shivered.

"Does this happen a lot?" Alicia asked sympathetically.

"Actually, I used to have nightmares often after I witnessed the murder. Until I went to Wyoming. Then they sort of stopped."

Now the trial had brought it all back. And there was no Mike to defend her, to hold her, to comfort her.

"I'm sorry I woke you. I've never had a nightmare more than once a night so shouldn't wake you up again," Savannah said. "But I'm keyed up. Maybe I'll read for a while. I can sit in the living room, so I don't keep you up with the light on."

"I can sleep with the lights on but use the living room if you want. Call if you need anything."

Alicia rose and gave a quick check around the living room before returning to the bedroom.

Savannah lit every light. She didn't want to go to sleep or think or remember. She wished Mike had been close. Wish he'd enclose her in his strong arms and never let her go.

Slowly she sank into the sofa and reached for the phone. The clock on the table displayed the hour in glowing red numerals: two-fifteen. With a quick glance to the bedroom door, she dialed the number Mike had given her when he left that evening.

"Black." The voice sounded crisp, alert.

"Mike, it's Savannah. Did I wake you up?"

"What's wrong?" Tension shimmered over the phone line.

"Nothing. Actually, I had another nightmare and woke Alicia up. She's gone back to bed now."

"You aren't supposed to call unless it's an emergency, I thought—Never mind what I thought," he said.

"I'm sorry I woke you up."

"Not a problem. You okay?"

"It was scary, but I'll be fine. Only, I didn't want to go back to sleep."

His voice warmed her to her toes. "I can understand that. You're afraid of another one."

"I thought I was over them after the last one at the ranch."

"This is your first nightmare since then, right? Probably brought on by seeing Ramirez today."

"Where are you staying?"

"Sam and I are sharing a room across the hall and down two doors."

"Did I wake him up, too?"

"No. He looked up once, then went back to sleep. Which is what you should do. We'll be there early in the morning to escort you to the courthouse."

"I know. I wish—"

What she wished for and what she was likely to get were two different things.

"What, baby?"

Her heart pounded at the soft endearment, at the husky, intimate tone in his voice.

"I wish we were still at the ranch."

"It'll all be over soon." His voice became gruff.

"I know. Sorry I woke you up."

She slipped the receiver back on the hook. She wanted kisses and caresses.

Mike wanted the case to end and to return home.

She wondered how she would survive that.

By the time Mike and Sam arrived the next morning, Alicia and Savannah were ready. Savannah wore a soft pink dress, and had pulled her hair back into a cascade of curls that skimmed her neck and tumbled down her back. She had done her best with makeup, but the dark circles were evident.

Mike commented on them as soon as he saw her.

"You didn't get back to sleep, did you?" he asked, tracing the delicate skin beneath her eyes.

"Not until almost morning," Savannah murmured.

He looked fine, better than fine. And she could have spent the day staring at him. His touch sent sparkling waves of sensation through her and she wanted to throw herself into his arms and have him hold her tightly.

"Let's roll, folks," Sam said.

Once back on the witness stand Savannah took Mike's advice and ignored Ramirez as much as she could. The district attorney questioned her in minute detail about that fateful evening. He had her trace her steps from that night, relate each scene until he had gleaned every bit of information. When he finished, it was the defense attorney's turn.

Savannah rubbed her hands together nervously and took a deep breath. She was halfway through. She only had to get through this cross-examination and it'd be finished. Darting a quick glance at Mike, she almost smiled at his thumbs-up sign. Then he smiled and her heart skidded. Facing the attorney, she knew she could do this.

The questions came fast and furiously as he tried to discredit her. She took her time in responding and more than once looked to Mike for reassurance, as if she could draw on his strength to meet this challenge. His steady gaze never left her.

When they recessed for lunch, Savannah still hadn't finished.

She ignored the glare and angry words whispered by Ramirez as she passed on her way to Mike. She had eyes only for the tall marshal and almost fell into his arms when she drew close.

"Well done, Savannah," he said warmly, his arm across her shoulder.

She glanced up and pressed closer as if seeking shelter. "That guy's awful."

"He's just doing his job, trying to defend the accused. Keep your facts simple, don't get flustered and you'll be finished in no time."

"Good work, Savannah."

Alicia joined them, her eyes darting back and forth between Savannah and Mike, speculation rampant. "Sam's brought lunch again. Let's go and relax. The defense attorney can't have too many more ways to ask if you're certain of what you saw that night. I think the judge is getting annoyed."

Savannah finished testifying at four. She was excused

from attending further court sessions unless recalled at a later date.

"I'm free?" she asked Alicia as they stood at the door to the courthouse.

Outside the sun shone bright and hot. The sound of the traffic was muted behind the heavy glass doors, but she saw the busy activity on the street

"You were never a prisoner," Alicia said, smiling.

"It sure felt like it sometimes."

Savannah held her breath, she didn't want to say good-bye to Mike here, on the steps of the courthouse, with Alicia and Sam standing by. She didn't want to say good-bye at all, but knew it was inevitable.

But not like this, please not like this.

"We'll watch you until the verdict's in. But the worst has been said today. I think the danger's past," Mike said.

Alicia nodded. "You should be safe enough to return home, pick up the pieces of your life. We'll be watching, but the word on the street is the deal's off if you testify, which you did today. Another scumbag off the streets."

She grinned at her fellow law enforcement colleagues. "Nice to meet you, Savannah. Good luck in the future."

"Thanks, Alicia. Thanks for keeping me safe."

"I'll see you to your place if you like," Mike said quietly. She nodded.

Smiling at Sam, she thanked him for his help.

"We'll get your clothes back to you tomorrow, no need for you to go by the hotel. Just head for home," Alicia said.

Mike hailed a cab and waited for Savannah to climb in. He followed her and gave the address to the taxi driver.

Silence stretched out between them as the cab careened

around corners and headed for Savannah's condo as if the driver was trying out for the Daytona Speedway. At one fast turn, she was thrown against Mike. Heat engulfed her and for a moment she was reluctant to move. But she straightened and looked away feeling flustered and shy.

"What will you do first?" Mike asked.

"What can I do?"

"Almost anything. The Miami office has officers scheduled to watch your house, follow you when you go to work or the store."

"Or the beach?"

He nodded.

"I guess I'll start with calling my boss to see if I still have a job," she replied promptly.

Glancing at her watch, she saw she could still reach Paulette at the boutique. Savannah hoped that Paulette hadn't hired someone else. She didn't know what she'd do if she didn't have her job. It'd help define who she was for years.

"And then?"

She looked at Mike. Why was he asking? Just to keep the silence at bay?

"Once the trial's over, once we know for sure he's not going to come after me, I want to go to the beach. I want to walk among people without wondering if someone's going to shoot me. I want to be outside all day and feel safe. I want to play in the surf, swim in the ocean, and eat a dozen hot dogs."

He smiled, his eyes watching her. "I know, you love junk food."

She nodded unable to look away. She loved junk food,

but not as much as she loved this man. She swallowed hard.

She didn't want to say good-bye.

"Want to come to the beach with me?" she asked one last time.

Mike hesitated, then shrugged. "If I get the assignment to watch you, I can stay one more day."

Her heart fluttered and pounded. She hoped the marshal service would let him stay. They'd have some more days together. Time to build memories, for her to discover more about him that she could remember down through the years.

When they pulled up before her apartment, Savannah followed Mike to the sidewalk. He scanned the area, settling on the dark sedan across the street. When the man behind the wheel nodded, Mike relaxed.

"Wait for me," he instructed the cabdriver

Disappointed he wasn't staying, Savannah led the way to her door. Her keys ready, she opened the door and stopped dead. The place smelled stale and musty. Her plants had died and now drooped sadly down the sides of their pots. Dust covered everything. It was home, yet it didn't feel like it.

"It normally looks nicer than this," she said softly, her eyes taking in every feature. It seemed small after the ranch house in Wyoming. It appeared feminine and cluttered after the sparsely furnished masculine decor of Tom Black's house.

But it was her home and she felt, at long last, safe.

"You've been away for months, Savannah. It probably looks a bit strange. But once you're back in the swing of things, everything will fall into place again. I'll try to pull the day shift and be by in the morning if that suit you?"

"Sure." She swung around to face him. "Mike, thank you

for everything. I mean, for protecting me, for showing me Wyoming and all."

For holding me in the night, for sharing that little bit of your life with me. I love you.

He pulled her into his arms and kissed her. She pressed against him, her blood surging as her arms encircled his neck and she pulled him closer. The dizzy sensations that flooded her gave her hope. He wasn't indifferent to her. He had to have some kind of feelings to kiss her so deeply.

Mike tangled his fingers in the fall of curls, winding the hair around his fingers, rubbing gently as he savored the feel of her silky hair. He angled his mouth for better access and swept his tongue inside to taste the honey sweetness that was Savannah.

The honking of the cab broke them apart.

"I'll be by in the morning."

He left so quickly Savannah reeled.

She stared at the retreating cab, unable to believe Mike could leave so abruptly.

Yet why shouldn't he? He'd never led her on. Never even hinted there could be something permanent between them. As much as he denied it, Savannah knew something connected them. Frustration built, and grief. He was too stubborn. He'd leave as soon as the trial was over and the verdict in. And end any chance they had to build a lasting love between them.

All because of Amy.

She wanted to scream, throw something, pound some sense into his head. If she were willing to take a chance after Robert, why couldn't he?

Unless, of course, there was nothing to take a chance on.

Was she some romantic fool, seeing something that didn't exist? Sure he'd kissed her a few times.

Men kissed women all the time, it didn't mean they wanted a forever relationship. She was an idiot if she thought so. She knew she was easy on the eyes, probably the kisses were his way of whiling away a boring assignment. With a deep sigh, she turned and headed for her bedroom. She had a phone call to make, a house to clean and a life to get back to.

Eleven days later Savannah heard the verdict. Joel Ramirez had been convicted of first degree murder and sentenced to life in prison without parole. Mike told her when he picked her up from work to drive her home.

He'd been successful in getting the day shift. He picked her up every morning and took her to the job that Paulette kept for her. He hung around the boutique area all day and drove her home in the late afternoons. Often staying for dinner, he wouldn't leave until his replacement knocked on the door.

"So I'm safe?" she asked upon hearing the verdict.

"We believe so. Tonight's the last night the marshal's service will post a guard. We think you're home free, Savannah," Mike said as he maneuvered her car through Miami rush hour traffic.

She swallowed, her heart tripping rapidly. "Are we still on for the beach, then? I'll take tomorrow off and we can go."

Over the days he'd been in Miami he'd built a high wall between them. After his kiss, he'd treated her impersonally, professionally. There'd been nothing personal between them, much as she wished there was.

Now his assignment was truly over.

"I'll go to the beach tomorrow, then head for home," he said as he stopped by her apartment.

She closed her eyes in relief. One more day.

When Mike knocked on her door the next morning, Savannah felt as shy as a schoolgirl. She'd donned her bathing suit and pulled on a T-shirt and shorts over. Her feet were shod in slip-on sandals. She'd pulled her hair away from her face and neck and it hung down in a swinging ponytail.

"Hi." She smiled brightly as she flung open the door, taking in the beloved features.

"Hi, yourself. Ready to go?"

Mike glanced over her from tousled curls to pink polish on her toes. He smiled in masculine appreciation.

Savannah flushed at his appraisal, feeling that shimmering sense of awareness, of longing that always surfaced when he was near.

"Yes. I brought a bunch of beach towels, some suntan lotion and snacks. We can get lunch at a stand by the beach." She looked away, feeling almost breathless.

"Junk food, of course," he murmured as she locked her door. "I have a car. We can take that if you like."

"You got a car? I thought we'd use mine."

"I'm booked on a 6:00 pm flight out, Savannah. I'll drop the car at the airport."

"Oh."

She'd known he was going home. Why the shock to hear

he was leaving at six?

"I could have dropped you at the airport."

"This is better," he said gently.

The beach was crowded, but Savannah found a spot that suited her near the water. The sun shone in a cloudless blue sky. The soothing sound of the surf provided a background to the shrieks and laughter of the children playing in the sand and the water's edge.

She gazed around at the crowd, men and women lying on towels, or sitting and talking. Children running, building sand castles, splashing and laughing. It was hectic, and so different from the quiet Wyoming ranch, Savannah looked at Mike.

Would he enjoy the day? Or were there too many people, too much commotion for him?

She frowned as she realized he scanned the beach as if he were searching for a wanted man.

"I thought I'd be safe," she said, dropping her beach bag and toeing off her sandals.

Over the last week she'd gradually become used to moving about, going to work, meeting strangers at the boutique without the constant fear.

His eyes swung round and met hers. "You are safe. We'd never have closed the case if we suspected anything different."

"Then why the search?" She gestured around the beach.

He smiled, and shrugged. "Habit."

"Oh."

Once again it pointed out the differences in their lives. She leaned over and withdrew a couple of large towels from her carryall. Handing one to him, she spread hers and then pulled off her top.

Mike took his towel and lay it down beside the one Savannah straightened out. When he stood, she had discarded her shirt. He swallowed at the sight of her brief bikini top. Her breasts were firm and high, the rounded tops glowing with honey-colored tan. Her shoulders were beautiful, her arms supple and firm. As she shimmied out of her shorts, he swallowed hard. She was gorgeous.

He'd known her figure was perfect from the times he'd held her. He'd seen her in a bathing suit at the ranch, but it had been conservative compared to this skimpy excuse. Her skin glowed in the sun and he wanted to pick her up and carry her somewhere private and make love to her all day long!

Was this her idea of trying to force something he was determined not to give? One look at her face convinced him it wasn't. She hadn't looked at him, wasn't trying to gauge his reaction, didn't throw flirtatious glances. She was genuinely excited to be at the beach for the day.

He realized there was little artifice about Savannah. She didn't flirt, she was naturally as friendly as a puppy. Her enthusiasm for everything shone from her face, even the events of the last few months hadn't dampened her exuberance for life.

"Can you swim?"

She turned to him, her bright smile almost melting his heart.

"Of course, did you forget the river? We swam in it a lot as kids."

"No one would ever forget the river. But wait until you

feel this water. This is for swimming, not freezing. Come on."

She almost danced as she hurried toward the surf.

Mike shucked his jeans, yanked his shirt over his head and set out to follow her, ignoring the feeling that convinced him the entire day would prove to be a mistake. For once he was going to enjoy the moment. He was leaving in a few hours.

And he knew in only a little while, Savannah would forget him.

They could both have today.

The ocean was as warm as a bath, the surf mild and invigorating. Frolicking like children, they played in the water, body surfing, water fighting, floating beyond the waves, riding the gentle swells.

"I love the beach," Savannah called at one point.

"Could have fooled me," Mike replied, coming up behind her and splashing water over her.

She laughed and turned, walloping a sheet of water right in his face. The fight started again until he thought she might drown if she didn't stop laughing so much.

Savannah finally had enough. She swam leisurely toward shore, standing when she reached the beach. Mike joined her seconds later.

"Had enough?" he asked, his eyes skimming over her.

"For now." She wrung the water from her hair and shook it, the ponytail slapping against her shoulders. The sun felt good. It was June and hot in Miami, not cool like it had been in Wyoming. For a moment she missed the mountains. She looked at the palm trees moving gracefully in the wind.

Happy to be home, she did miss the west. How odd,

she'd only been there for three weeks. Yet it had earned a place in her heart.

"Lunch now?" Mike asked as they walked to their towels.

"Yes, then a long tanning session."

She smiled at him, suddenly aware of how fleeting time was. In only a few hours he'd be leaving. The minutes flew by and she could do nothing to stop them.

Even out of cowboy boots, he walked like a cowboy, Savannah mused as they climbed to the boardwalk and headed toward a hot dog stand. Arrogant, confident, almost cocky. His chest was tanned dark as teak, with just a dusting of black hair that sparkled with droplets of salt water. His long legs were strong, covered with a similar dusting of dark hair. Her fingers longed to brush across the defined muscles, test their strength, knowing how hard and fit he was.

She noticed more than one woman gave a second look as they walked by. Feeling both smug Mike walked with her, and jealous of the glances he garnered, she tilted her chin a bit. No one was going to lasso this cowboy, but for today, he was with her.

"You want a hot dog?" he asked as they reached the stand.

"I want two with mustard and relish. And a large iced tea," she said, standing close enough to scent the mix of salt and sea and man.

Her eyes traced every inch of exposed skin, memorizing him. Unable to stop herself, her fingertips ran down his muscular arm, tingling in response. Mike turned and looked at her, his eyes narrowed, his gaze intense.

She took a breath and turned to the concessionaire.

Smiling at the man, she reached for her hot dogs, balanced them both in one hand as she took her drink. Mike bought two for himself and a drink. In minutes they were back at the towels.

"What happened with the deal to buy into the boutique ? You haven't mentioned it," he asked as Savannah took the first bite.

She closed her eyes, savoring every bit of flavor. It'd been months since she'd had a beach hot dog. Nothing tasted as good.

"You knew the marshal's office told her I'd be back. So Paulette's still willing to discuss partnership. She said as soon as the trial was over. I expect we'll talk about it more tomorrow."

"That must have been a relief."

Somehow she didn't feel as strongly about buying in as she once had. Probably delayed reaction to all that happened.

Mike glanced at his watch and Savannah's heart sank. She didn't want to know how much time they had left. She wanted to pretend that this day could last forever.

When she finished her lunch, Savannah rummaged in her beach bag and brought forth the sun screen. "Want some? Your legs might get burned. How come you're so dark on your chest and not your legs?" She held out the plastic bottle.

Mike took it and spread lotion on his legs. Her eyes watched every movement, wishing she'd offered to spread it on.

"I might ride a horse with no shirt in the summer, but I sure wouldn't ride without jeans."

"Do you spend a lot of time at the ranch?" she asked.

"Not a lot. Holidays, vacations. Tom runs the place. I help out from time to time."

"Ummm."

She still had a thousand questions, but knew he wouldn't answer them. He kept his life private. And maybe it was better.

It had taken her a long time to get over Robert. Maybe without knowing any more about Mike, she could put him behind her faster and get on with her life.

"Want me to spread some on your back?" he asked.

"Okay."

She turned partway around and presented her back. The lotion felt cool, but only for a second. Then his palms spread it over her skin and the tingling sparks of sensation heated her like a second sun. She closed her eyes to better relish the feel of Mike's touch, his fingers and palm roughened a bit from the work on the ranch. Still his hands were warm and gentle, sweeping over her shoulders, down the long length of her spine, over the top of her hips. Up again.

Suddenly tears filled her eyes, trickled down her cheeks. She held her breath, afraid he'd notice. He was good at noticing.

"Savannah?"

He turned her face toward his.

She opened her eyes and gazed at him, trying to smile, but her lips trembled and she was afraid she'd burst into sobs if she pushed it.

"Did I hurt you?"

Not yet, but he would—when he left this afternoon. She shook her head, blinking rapidly, trying to dissipate the tears.

"I'm going to miss you, Mike," she said softly, her hand reaching out to rest on his shoulder.

They were so close, his breath skimmed across her cheeks. She could see the dark blue of the Miami sky and Mike's eyes.

His hands cupped her face, his thumbs brushed away the tears.

"In a week you'll forget all about me, I promise," he said softly.

She clamped her fingers over his wrists, and shook her head. "I don't think so, Mike. I don't think I'll ever forget you."

"I've been through this before, Savannah, I know what I'm talking about."

"And if you're wrong, then what?"

"I'm not." He was sure, he'd been through this once before. "Do you want to leave now?"

She shook her head, rubbing her fingers against his forearm. "No, I want to lie in the sun and hear the surf and feel the salty breeze. You've got a few hours, stay until it's time to go to the airport."

"Fine." He released her and settled back on his towel. Savannah lay on her stomach, cradling her face against one arm, her eyes on him. The minutes ticked by, faster and faster.

When he rolled over to look at her sometime later, Savannah was almost asleep.

"Hey, want to go in for one last swim?"

Her eyes flicked open and she smiled. "If you want."

"For a while. I have to get you home and get back to the hotel to shower before leaving for the airport. We have a little time, though."

Not long enough to suit her, she thought as they walked down to the water's edge. Never long enough to suit her.

They swam and body surfed, but the fun had faded for Savannah. Each beat of her heart signaled another second gone. Soon all the seconds left to them would be gone and he'd leave. She tried to hold on to time, but it proved impossible.

At last they walked ashore and dried off.

It took only ten minutes to reach her apartment. Feeling sick with trepidation, Savannah tried to smile as she licked dry lips. "I don't suppose you want to come in?" she asked.

"I don't have time."

"Right. I'm glad you stayed for the day. Thanks again for everything."

She opened the car door.

"Savannah, trust me in this. I know what I'm talking about." Mike stayed her with a hand on her arm.

"Maybe. Time will tell, won't it?" She blinked hard, determined not to cry—at least until she was alone.

He pulled her closer and kissed her—his mouth warm and firm and demanding. His lips moved against hers, opening hers. His touch inflamed. Savannah leaned against him, savoring, treasuring each second. Her tongue met his and dared him to leave. Her mouth moved, demanded in return. Her hands clutched in near desperation as the kiss spiraled them higher and higher.

She loved this man so much she wanted to burst. And her heart threatened just that, when he put her away from him. Brushing his fingertips across her mouth he smiled a sad smile. Her heart racing, it was all she could do not to grab hold and never let go.

"Have a nice life, baby," he said softly.

"Bye, Mike." She slid from the car and walked on wobbly knees to her front door. As the key turned, she heard the car pull away. But she didn't look back. There was nothing there.

Eleven

By the end of the first week Savannah knew Mike had been wrong. She missed him more than even she'd expected. And her feelings had not changed, diminished nor faded.

Throwing herself into work helped keep her mind from dwelling on him, but the enthusiasm she'd once felt was missing. She went through the motions every day, doing what needed to be done, filling her hours, but it felt like a chore.

When Paulette inquired if she were still interested in buying into the boutique, Savannah was unable to answer immediately.

"Could I let you know in another day or two?" she asked.

Amazed at her response, she felt relief when her boss agreed. Savannah had pushed hard for the deal only seven months earlier, had thought part ownership the cumulation of all her dreams. Now she hesitated. Her interest had changed.

Restless, she couldn't remain in the boutique during her breaks and took to walking during her lunch hour.

Each time she saw a tall, tanned, dark-haired man, her heart lurched until she verified it wasn't Mike. Her mind knew he wasn't in Miami, but her heart kept hope and she couldn't stop looking for him in every man she saw. She wondered what he was doing. Was he guarding another witness or hunting a fugitive?

Had he forgotten her or was he thinking about her as much as she thought about him?

Nothing held her attention for long.

She lost weight.

And every night she dreamed of Mike Black. The nightmares had ended, instead her dreams now teemed with excitement, like the man himself. And they emphasized his absence, making her miss him all the more.

At the end of the month, Paulette called Savannah into her small office one afternoon and shut the door firmly.

"All right, Savannah. Time to talk."

"About the business?"

Savannah still hadn't made up her mind about buying. She couldn't understand her lethargy, but it seemed too big a decision to make. She sank in the chair opposite Paulette and idly gazed at the papers on the polished desk. She knew such waffling wouldn't help her, but she couldn't work up any enthusiasm.

"Not about the business, about you. I know your life's been on a roller coaster since you saw the murder, but it's time to get back on track. The trial is over. Ramirez is locked away for good. Your life's no longer being threatened. I know it's hard, but you have to put the turmoil and fear behind you and get going again."

Savannah looked at her. "I have."

"No. Something's still missing from the Savannah Adams I knew. You have lost so much weight your clothes hang on you. You constantly have circles under your eyes. You smile at the customers, but never joke around with the other employees. And the drive you had to push to the top is missing. What's wrong?"

Savannah shifted her gaze to the small window high in the back wall. From that rectangle, all she could see was blue sky. Like the blue sky over Wyoming. Her gaze dropped back down to meet Paulette's.

"Isn't it enough that my entire life was disrupted for over six months?" she asked quietly.

Paulette shook her head. Tapping her long nails on the polished desk, she studied the younger woman. "You're a fighter and a survivor. I know how you worked your way through college, fought to move up in the business. You've been back a month, time enough to regain your enthusiasm and zest for life. Yet you seem worse now than when you first returned. There's something else. What?"

Savannah sighed and met Paulette's eyes. "I fell for one of the marshals guarding me."

She took pleasure in admitting it aloud even while the ache of missing him threatened to overwhelm her.

Paulette nodded in satisfaction. "I knew there had to be more. And my guess would be it was that good-looking one who came to the office for a couple of weeks while the trial was going on. Well, what happened?"

Savannah shrugged. "He didn't fall for me," she said simply. "At least, he says he didn't."

She remembered his kisses, his protectiveness, his jealousy about the other cowboys on the Bar B. He had to have felt something for her!

"And?"

"And I wish I believed him. He'd been burned once before and was unwilling to take a chance with me."

It hurt more than she'd expected. Time hadn't softened the blow.

Paulette gave her a dry look. "So what are you going to do about it? Pine away until you're skin and bones?"

Savannah shook her head, straightened her shoulders and tilted her chin. "I'm doing okay."

"Okay isn't how you used to live your life. The Savannah who badgered me into considering selling part of my business wouldn't let this get her down. She'd fight back. The Savannah who increased our customer base with her wonderful smile and enthusiasm wouldn't stand around moping for a month. She'd find a way to make the sale."

"How?"

Selling Mike on taking a chance wasn't quite like selling a dress to a tourist.

Paulette smiled and leaned back in her chair.

"Come on, Savannah, you're a determined successful woman. You don't need me to tell you how to go after something you want. If you truly want this man, do something about it. Or cut him out of your life. But stop this moping around."

Savannah stared at her. Had she been moping around? Thinking over the last few weeks, she knew she'd focused entirely on how much she missed Mike.

Paulette was right, she was a fighter. Time she fought back.

No guts, no glory, Steve had said.

And she deserved the glory of having Mike share her life. They both did. Could she convince him of that?

Standing with a surge of enthusiasm, Savannah slowly smiled at Paulette, her eyes beginning to dance.

"You're right, Paulette. I may need a few days off."

"Now wait a minute. I didn't mean for you to take time off. You just had six months off, now you want another few days?" Paulette seemed flabbergasted Savannah would even ask.

"Yes, I do. And when I get back we'll talk about my buying into the business. I picked up a few ideas from some places I saw in Laramie. I've got a great idea for a Christmas special that will bring in hoards of customers. But first, I have to get some things straight with a certain U.S. marshal!"

Savannah hurried home. She loved him. She remained certain of her feelings and suspected he could love her in return if he'd let go of Amy's betrayal. Once that was behind them, could they have a chance at building a life together?

She wasn't sure how, or even where, just yet. She loved Miami, never thought to live anywhere else. But she'd do it to be with Mike. She knew he loved Colorado and Wyoming. Could he ever be happy in Miami?

Surely they could work something out if they both wanted to be together.

First she had to convince him she loved him, that it wasn't infatuation, nor some stupid syndrome. And find out if he could love her.

Honestly, that man could be very dense sometimes!

Or, had she read him wrong? Was he truly not interested in her? Had his kisses and caresses been a way to pass the time?

No, she didn't believe that. He wasn't the type, nor would he have stayed that last day in Miami if he hadn't wanted to spend time with her.

Reaching her apartment, she hurried to the phone. In less than a half hour, her plans were made. Scheduled to leave for Colorado the next morning, she slowly sank back against her chair, her heart racing with anticipation and fear.

She hoped she wasn't making a monumental mistake. The entire situation could blow up into her face. Betting the ranch on a hunch was one thing. This was her pride at stake—and her future.

Savannah slid into the driver's seat of the rental car and slammed the door. Couldn't anything be easy? she fumed as she snapped the key to start the engine. Pulling out into traffic, she followed the directions she'd been given and before long turned onto the highway leading from Denver to Fort Collins and then Wyoming.

Mike hadn't been home. The first setback.

She found the address for the marshals' office in the phone book and paid a visit only to discover he had vacation coming and had taken it.

Frustrated with the delay, she headed the car north.

He always took his vacation at the ranch.

She'd find him there—at least she'd better. Having made up her mind, she chafed at the delay. She wanted to find him and—

And what? It was one thing to face the man in the privacy of his apartment. She wasn't at all sure she was up to facing him in front of all the men who worked the ranch. And his brother and new sister-in-law would be there, as well.

Sighing, Savannah turned on the radio. She'd just have to make do with whatever situation she found. Paulette was right, she was a fighter and this time fighting for the most important thing in her life.

The day was fresh and clear, with a steady breeze from the west. The grass was drying, the green interspersed with brown, but still plentiful. The two-lane road from Fort Collins cut through rolling hills. Cattle grazed peacefully in sections, reminding her of similar stretches on the Bar B.

Memories assailed Savannah: her reluctance when she'd first come to Wyoming in protective custody, how tired she'd been; how upset to be stashed on a Western ranch instead of a beach in California.

In retrospect, that had been three of the most wonderful weeks of her life. But not because of the location, because of the man who kept her safe.

He was an idiot, just like they said, Mike thought as he tossed a shirt toward the flight bag on his bed. It caught on the edge, slid onto the bedspread. Frowning, he snatched it up and thrust it into the bag.

Hank had said it first, when Mike arrived at the ranch without Savannah, telling everyone the engagement was over.

He never should have started the charade in the first place. He could trust the men on the ranch. The truth would have sufficed, and then he wouldn't have to put up with their constant comments about what a fool he'd been to let her go.

He should have told them the truth when he'd shown

up without her. But he hadn't wanted them to know he'd lied to them about Savannah. They were good men, deserved more than that. So he'd put up with their sly comments, questions, and advice.

Glancing around, he had everything he wanted—two changes of clothes, his shaving kit. He snapped the flight bag closed and picked it up.

It might be a long time before he came back to the ranch for vacation. He didn't need to have everyone from Steve to his own brother watching him and shaking their heads in disgust.

Not that their comments had been the worst of it. Everywhere he looked, he saw Savannah, from the corral where she'd learned to ride, to the front yard where he'd stopped her sunbathing. Even the guest room across the hall held memories he couldn't expunge in passing.

Was she all right? Had she picked up the pieces of her life and gone on as if the last year had never existed? Did she ever think about him?

What if you're wrong, Mike? What if I don't forget?

Mike headed his Jeep toward Denver. He'd come to the ranch for some solitude and a time to think. Instead he'd caught grief from everyone. He'd be home by dark, and if he didn't change his mind, he'd put part two of his plan into motion tomorrow. He had until then to come to his senses.

Maybe a quick trip to Miami would show that he'd been right to leave in the first place. Even though Savannah proved different than Amy, it didn't mean that he should consider marriage. It didn't mean they'd find anything different from what his father had with his many marriages.

He shook his head. That wasn't true. Savannah was

different. And she'd wrapped herself around his heart. He wanted to see her smiles, watch those blue eyes light up in delight, hear her Southern drawl, taste her lips and feel that feminine body snuggled up to his.

It'd be a gamble. And he had until tomorrow to decide if he was willing to risk it.

The two-lane road from Laramie to Fort Collins was practically deserted. The interstate was to the east and most drivers wanted the convenience and speed that the freeway offered. The rolling hills and curves of the Fort Collins road didn't offer much speed, but Mike didn't mind He had no deadline to meet. Still had a few days left on his vacation. And no plans for the rest of today. Tomorrow was a different story. But he'd worry about that decision later.

Cresting a hill, he slowed when he saw the vehicles bunched in the distance. Must be a bad accident, there were a half dozen trucks lined up at the side of the road. As he drove closer, he noticed the trucks were parked on the shoulder. He counted eight. Passing, he noticed a small sedan jacked up, a cowboy changing the tire while others hung around, probably giving unneeded advice.

Slamming on his brakes, Mike whipped his head around and caught a glimpse of frothy blond curls, a bright red dress and long tanned legs that didn't quit. He yanked his Jeep to the graveled shoulder and cut his engine. Slamming the door shut, he quickly strode across the asphalt right into the midst of the group of cowboys and the one blond bombshell he knew too well.

Her hair shone like sunshine. She should have pulled it back into a ponytail and shoved it under a hat. Instead it swirled around her face, framing the sparkling eyes. Her smile seemed as big as Wyoming, and each cowboy there hung on her every word.

His eyes ran over every inch of her stopping at the short sassy skirt that needed another twelve inches to make it respectable. Then he traced those long legs and the sexy high heeled shoes showcasing her dainty feet.

He didn't blame the men surrounding her for hovering like bees around a flower. It seemed to be a normal state of events around Savannah. And she seemed as oblivious about it as she had on the Bar B.

Her friendliness showed no bounds nor gender. She'd been just as friendly, open, enthusiastic with Alicia and Paulette.

But that didn't mean he wanted every cowboy in Wyoming around her.

Jealousy burned deep.

He wanted her smiles.

He wanted her laughter.

He wanted her!

He didn't need tomorrow to consider his decision, it was made.

"Need some help?" he asked.

Savannah turned and the sight of the gladness in her eyes shocked him to his heels.

"Mike!"

She took three running steps and threw herself against his chest, her arms coming around his neck, holding on so tight he thought she'd strangle him.

Without thinking, he caught her close and lowered his mouth to hers. Dimly he grew aware of the groans of the other men, but he didn't stop kissing her. It'd been too long and he felt duty bound to make up for lost time.

She was so soft and sweet, the air was filled with honeysuckle. His arms were filled with the feminine bundle of energy he'd missed so much.

Savannah opened her mouth to Mike's and reveled in the sensations splashing through her. When his arms closed tightly around her, she knew she'd come home. His hot kiss confirmed it. He had to feel something for her, this proved it She never wanted to move again. For once something worked out right!

He broke the kiss and held her back, his eyes skimming over her as if he could devour her. "You're skin and bones."

"I'm so glad to see you," Savannah murmured, her eyes alight in happiness.

He was big and solid and still caused her heart to kick into high gear.

"What kind of trouble are you in now?" His gaze scanned the men, some grumbling as they backed toward their trucks, the cowboy changing the tire finished, pounding on the hubcap.

"I had a flat tire and all these nice men stopped to help me. Do you know Shorty Gates?"

She looked over her shoulder and smiled at the man who'd just finished. "I couldn't have managed without his help, and everyone else's."

She smiled at the group and to a man they smiled back, but she made no move to leave Mike's arms.

"I love Wyoming. Everyone's so friendly. I could have been stranded for hours out here."

"Not likely," Mike muttered. He nodded to the men. "Appreciate your stopping to help her out. I can take care of her from here."

Keeping her firmly in the circle of his arm, he watched as the others said farewell and ambled to their trucks. In less than five minutes he and Savannah stood alone on the side of the road.

"I might have known the next time I'd see you, there'd be a dozen men surrounding you," he said as the last truck pulled away.

"I'm happy to see you, too, Mike."

Her hands rubbed his shoulders, her fingers tingling, her eyes taking in every inch of his beloved face. He looked tired. Had he lost weight, too?

Had he missed her?

"What are you doing here?"

Mike held her away, his hands gripping her shoulders as he stared down into her face, a scowl on his own.

"I love you, Mike. I told you that before. And more than a week is up. It's been a month. I still feel the same, so I thought I'd make sure you knew it. Maybe we need to talk, cowboy. I'm not Amy," she said bravely.

His eyes softened and he drew her closer, hugging her, resting his cheek on her soft froth of hair.

"I know you're not Amy. She never gave me the trouble you do."

He cupped her face with his palms and tipped it up to meet his lips. They were soft, gentle, loving.

"I've been a total idiot, according to everyone on the ranch. I was on my way to Miami to see you. Maybe ask you out to dinner or something. What you said that night about what if I was wrong just kept replaying in my head. So I thought I'd see if you felt the same. I couldn't stay away," he said against her mouth.

She laughed in sheer happiness. "You were coming to Miami? Imagine if we'd passed on the road and I ended up at the ranch and you ended up at my apartment." She shivered. "That's too close. If you hadn't been here, I'm not sure I would have been brave enough to track you down again."

"I'd have come for you, Savannah. I wanted to know for sure if your feelings lasted. You worked your way into my heart until I feel incomplete without you."

"In the meantime we've had weeks apart because of your stupid worries." She held on to his wrists as she gazed up into his eyes. "I'm not Amy. I tried to tell you that before."

"I should mention that I hate a woman who says she told me so."

"Learn to live with it, Marshal. If I'm right, I like to brag about it," she said sassily, love spilling out.

"Brag all you want, sweetheart, these last few weeks have been horrible. Everyone at the ranch accused me of being an idiot for letting you go. And they were right. Everywhere I looked, I saw you. Every word you spoke echoed in my mind. At night I dreamed of you. It's hard to overcome a long-held belief, but my need for you in my life outweighs my reservations. I need you to be sure. As I needed to be sure. What I feel for you is nothing like what I felt for Amy or any other woman. I am not my father. I want you with me for the rest of our lives. Marry me, Savannah. Give me your smiles for the rest of your life. Come live with me, share with me. Have babies with me. Grow old with me."

"Are you sure, Mike? Oh, please be sure. I want to very much, but there's so much to consider. I love you, but I love Miami. While Wyoming's great, once I got used to it, I don't think I want to live here always. I truly love the beach. And you like the west. I wouldn't ask you to give that up for me. But I'm not sure a long distance relationship would work, either."

"I've been thinking about Galveston. It's in Texas, on the Gulf, with some of the world's best beaches. You'd be by the water, I'd be in a place I could be comfortable in. You could start your own dress shop. I'll work out of the local marshal's office. What do you think?" he asked, his eyes serious, his hands warm and loving as he awaited her answer.

Tears welled, but she blinked them away. This wasn't a spur of the moment thing. He hadn't stopped because he'd seen her on the side of the road. He'd thought far enough ahead to plan a compromise for their home. He'd been on his way to Miami to find her, tell her he loved her. She'd never been so happy.

"Yes, please, of course I'll marry you. I love you."

His eyes gazed down into hers and he smiled. Her heart flipped over at the dimple and she inched a finger over to touch it.

"I love you, sweetheart, I always will."

He'd get use to her bubbly ways, her sunny smile, her friendly attitude. He'd have to share her with others, but at least she'd be his alone at night.

And the future looked exciting once he knew he'd share

it with Savannah.

His brother hadn't let his father's mistakes rule his life.

Nor would Mike. He'd take a chance with this woman. And never let her go. It was the best move he'd ever make.

This love was forever. Lowering his head, his mouth covered hers in a kiss of bright promise.

If you liked **Cowboy Marshal,**
you'll love the next book in the *Cowboy Hero* series,
Summer Cowboy.

If you enjoyed **Cowboy Marshal**
please consider leaving a review.

More Books by Barbara McMahon

Cowboy Hero Series
The Cowboy Next Door
Cowboy's Bride
One Stubborn Cowboy
Crazy About a Cowboy
Never Doubt a Cowboy
Cowboy Marshal
Summer Cowboy
Second Chance Cowboy
Movie Star Cowboy

Cowboys of Wildcat Creek
Valentine's Cowboy Rescue
Shelly and the Cowboy
Kristi's Cowboy Hero
Holly's Reluctant Cowboy
A Cowboy for Eliza

Sweet Reunion Romance Collection
Unexpected Reunion
Unpredictable Reunion
Unanticipated Reunion

The Harts of Texas Series
Rebel Heart
Tangled Hearts
Reckless Heart

Ultimate Billionaires Series
The Cynical Sheikh
Falling for the Sheikh
A Sheikh of Her Own
The Unforgettable Sheikh

Rocky Point Series
Rocky Point Legacy
Rocky Point Reunion
Rocky Point Promise
Rocky Point Hero
Rocky Point Inn
Rocky Point Dawn

The Talmadge Sisters Series
Letters to Caroline
Michelle's Marriage Deal
Trusting Abby

Tropical Escapes Series
Island Rendezvous
Come into the Sun
Island Paradise

A Sweet Clean Christmas Romance Collection
The Christmas Cop
The Cowboy's Special Christmas
A Soldier's Christmas
A Teaspoon of Mistletoe
The Christmas Locket
A Key West Christmas

Sweet Romance Stand-alone Collection
Because of You
Cowboy Charade
I'll Take Forever
Jared's Promise
Mail Order Bride
Not Really Married
Sweet Meant To Be
The Cowboy Comes Home
The Paper Marriage
Trusting Jake
The Banished Bride